Out of Control

RACHEL YODER—
Always Trouble Somewhere

Book 3

WANDA *&*
BRUNSTETTER

BARBOUR
PUBLISHING

Cover artist: Richard Hoit

For more information about Wanda E. Brunstetter, please access the author's Web site at the following Internet address: www.wandabrunstetter.com

Published by Barbour Publishing, Inc., P.O. Box 719, Uhrichsville, Ohio 44683, www.barbourbooks.com

Our mission is to publish and distribute inspirational products offering exceptional value and biblical encouragement to the masses.

ecpa Member of the
Evangelical Christian
Publishers Association

Printed in the United States of America.

Dedication

To the students and teachers at the Honeybrook School
in Topeka, Indiana. Thanks for letting me visit with you!

Other books by Wanda E. Brunstetter

Fiction

Rachel Yoder—Always Trouble Somewhere Series
> *School's Out!*
> *Back to School*
> *New Beginnings*

Sisters of Holmes County Series
> *A Sister's Secret*
> *A Sister's Test*
> *A Sister's Hope*

Brides of Webster County Series
> *Going Home*
> *On Her Own*
> *Dear to Me*
> *Allison's Journey*

Daughters of Lancaster County Series
> *The Storekeeper's Daughter*
> *The Quilter's Daughter*
> *The Bishop's Daughter*

Brides of Lancaster County Series
> *A Merry Heart*
> *Looking for a Miracle*
> *Plain and Fancy*
> *The Hope Chest*

Nonfiction

> *Wanda Brunstetter's Amish Friends Cookbook*
> *The Simple Life*

Glossary

ach—oh
aldi—girlfriend
appeditlich—delicious
baremlich—terrible
bauchweh—stomachache
bensel—silly child
blappermaul—blabbermouth
bletsching—spanking
boppli—baby
bruder—brother
buwe—boy
daed—dad
danki—thank you
dappich—clumsy
dumm—dumb
ekelhaft—disgusting
grank—sick
guder mariye—good morning
gut—good
hund—dog
jah—yes
kapp—cap
kinner—children
koppweh—headache
kumme—come
maedel—girl
mamm—mom
maus—mouse
melassich—molasses
mupsich—stupid

retschbeddi—tattletale
schmaert—smart
schnee—snow
schneeballe—snowball
schnell—quickly
schweschder—sister
ungeduldich—impatient
verhuddelt—mixed up
wasserpareble—chicken pox
wunderbaar—wonderful

Halt ei, sell geht zu weit!—Stop, that's going too far!
Sis nau futsch!—It's all ruined now!
Dummel dich net!—Take your time, don't hurry!
Gern gschehne.—You are welcome.

Contents

Chapter 1
Sledding Troubles

W*oosh. . . Woosh. . .* The wind whistled under the eaves of the house, rattling Rachel Yoder's bedroom window.

Thump-thumpety-thump! Rachel's heart pounded inside her chest. She shivered and pulled the quilt under her chin. She had thought she was getting less afraid of storms. But it was hard to be brave in a dark room with the wind making strange noises. What if the windows broke? What if the tree outside her bedroom window toppled and crashed onto the house?

Rachel closed her eyes and prayed, "Dear God, protect this house and all of us in it. Help me not be afraid."

Rachel drew in a deep breath. She felt a bit calmer, and her heart wasn't beating so fast. Maybe now she could sleep.

Tap-tap. Tap-tap.

Rachel's heart raced again. She tipped her head toward the window and listened. *Tap-tap. Tap-tap.* Was someone knocking on the glass? Had they climbed the tree outside her window? Were they trying to enter her room?

My imagination is just playing tricks on me. The wind is just blowing a tree branch against the window.

Screech. . . Screech. . . The new sound reminded Rachel of fingernails on a blackboard.

There's no reason to be afraid, she told herself. *God is watching over me.*

Rachel pushed the quilt aside, turned on the flashlight she kept by her bed, and plodded across the chilly wood floor. She lifted the dark green window shade and pressed her forehead against the cold glass.

Screech. . . Screech. Tap-tap. . .tap-tap.

Rachel gasped when she saw a small pink paw flopped against the window.

"Cuddles!"

She quickly opened the window, and a gust of cold wind swept into the room. "You silly kitten! What are you doing in that tree on such a cold, snowy night?"

Cuddles's pathetic *meow* was drowned out by the wooshing wind.

Snowflakes swirled into the room. Rachel picked up the cat and shut the window. "Poor Cuddles," she whispered against the cat's frosty head. "Did you get locked out of the barn?"

Cuddles meowed again and licked Rachel's chin with her sandpaper tongue.

Rachel giggled. "You're sure getting heavy, Cuddles. Before long you'll be a full-grown cat."

Meow!

"Do you want to sleep with me tonight?"

Meow! Meow! Cuddles pushed her paws against Rachel's chest and purred.

"You're getting me all wet!" Rachel felt the cold dampness through her nightgown and shivered. She plucked a small blanket from the doll cradle Pap had made her last Christmas. Then she wrapped Cuddles in the blanket and placed her at the foot of the bed.

Rachel was about to crawl back in bed, when Cuddles wriggled free from the blanket, leaped into the air, and landed on Rachel's pillow. The cat purred as she kneaded the pillow, first with one paw and then the other.

"Stop that!" Rachel scolded. "You're getting my pillow wet!" She picked up the cat, wrapped her in the doll blanket again, and placed her back on the end of the bed. "Now go to sleep, and I'll see you in the morning."

Rachel crawled into bed and pulled the quilt under her chin. The howling wind didn't bother her nearly so much now that Cuddles was near. She closed her eyes and was almost asleep when she heard *screech. . .screech. . .*

Her eyes popped open and she sat straight up. Cuddles was scratching a bedpost.

"Don't do that! You'll mark up my bed." Rachel pushed the covers aside and climbed out of bed. She wrapped Cuddles in the doll blanket and placed her at the end of the bed. "Now go to sleep."

Rachel was about to climb into bed again, when Cuddles sprang off the bed, slid across the floor, and bit into the shoelaces from one of Rachel's shoes. She flipped her head from side to side. *Bump. . .bump. . . bump. . .*the shoe thudded against the hardwood floor.

"*Shh. . .* If you're not careful, you'll wake Mom and Pap." Rachel grabbed the shoe and put it in her closet. Then she picked up Cuddles and put her on the bed. "If you make me get up again, I'll put you back outside."

Meow! Cuddles tipped her head and looked at Rachel as if to say, *"I'll be good. Please, don't put me in the cold."*

"All right then." Sighing, Rachel got into bed, pulled the quilt up to her chin, and closed her eyes. She listened for several minutes, but all was quiet. Cuddles must have finally gone to sleep.

When Rachel woke up the next morning, she rushed to the window and lifted the shade. The wind had stopped howling and the snow had quit falling. A perfect day for sledding!

Rachel thought about her new friend, Orlie. He'd told her that he thought the new sled he'd gotten for Christmas was the fastest around.

"We'll see about that," Rachel murmured as she slipped her nightgown over her head. "I'll bet my trusty old sled will go faster than Orlie's shiny new one. He just likes to brag."

She opened her closet door and took out a long-sleeved dress. "I'd better dress warmly today if I'm going to race my sled during recess."

After dressing, Rachel hurried downstairs to the kitchen. Mom was in front of their gas-operated stove, stirring a pot of oatmeal. The spicy aroma of cinnamon tickled Rachel's nose and made her stomach rumble.

"*Guder mariye* [good morning], Rachel," Mom said with a cheery smile.

"Good morning, Mom."

"Did you sleep well last night?"

"The wind kept me awake at first, and then after I brought—" Rachel clamped her hand over her mouth. She had almost blurted out that she'd let Cuddles into her room.

"What's the matter?" Mom asked, squinting her blue eyes. "Why are you covering your mouth?"

Rachel dropped her hand. "Nothing's wrong. I slept okay. How about you, Mom?"

"Except for your *daed's* [dad's] snoring, I slept fairly well, too." Mom touched her stomach and smiled. "I guess I should get used to not sleeping so much. When the *boppli* [baby] is born in July, I'll be up several times during the night to feed the little one."

Rachel grimaced. She wasn't sure she wanted a new baby in the house. What if Mom and Pap loved the baby more than they loved her? What if she had to do more chores after the baby came?

"Would you please set the table?" Mom asked, touching Rachel's arm.

"*Jah* [yes], okay." Rachel reached into the cupboard to get the glasses, but her elbow bumped the box of brown sugar on the cupboard. The box tumbled to the floor, and—*splat!*—brown sugar spilled everywhere.

"Always trouble somewhere," Rachel muttered. "I'll clean it up right away, Mom." She hurried to the cleaning closet for the broom and dustpan.

Swish! Swish! She swept sugar into the dustpan. *Swish! Swish!* Just a few more sweeps and it would be done.

Rachel bent over to pick up the dustpan, when— *woosh!*—a gray-and-white ball of fur streaked into the room. The dustpan flew out of Rachel's hand, and brown sugar flew everywhere. Some even landed on Cuddles's head.

"Oh no," Rachel said with a groan.

"What's that cat doing in the house?" Mom rubbed the spot on her nose where her metal-framed glasses should have been. Instead, they had slipped to the end of her nose. "I wonder if one of the men left the back door open when they went to do their chores," she said, pushing her glasses back in place.

Rachel frowned. Come to think of it, she hadn't seen Cuddles on her bed this morning. The silly kitten must have hidden so she wouldn't be put out in the cold.

Rachel knew Mom didn't like Cuddles to be in her room—especially not on the bed. She wondered what she could tell Mom that wouldn't be a lie. Should she admit that she'd let Cuddles into her room last night, or should she let Mom think the cat had entered through an open door this morning? Maybe it would be best if she just kept quiet.

"However the cat got in," Mom said, "she's caused a mess. The troublesome creature needs to go back outside, *schnell* [quickly]."

"I'll put her out." Rachel scooped Cuddles into her arms, opened the back door, and set the cat on the porch. "You'd better go out to the barn now." She shook her finger. "And if you don't stop getting into trouble, Mom might not let you in the house anymore."

"Why didn't you bring your sled this morning?" Rachel asked her brother Jacob as she trudged through the snow, pulling her sled toward the schoolhouse.

"Don't feel like sledding." Jacob kicked at a clump of snow with the toe of his boot.

"Are you afraid my sled might beat yours in a race? Is that why you left it in the barn?"

Jacob shook his head.

"Then why didn't you bring it?"

"I just told you. . .I don't feel like sledding today."

"How come?"

"You ask too many questions, little *bensel* [silly child]."

"I'm not a silly child. Will you ever stop calling me that?"

"Maybe someday. . .when we're both old and gray."

Rachel frowned. "Very funny."

Jacob reached down and scooped up a handful of snow. He waited until Rachel walked past him, then *splat!*—the cold, wet snow hit the collar of Rachel's coat. Some ran down her neck.

Rachel shivered and glared at Jacob. "I think someone ought to wash your face in the snow!"

"Who's gonna do it?" Jacob taunted. "*You*, little bensel?"

Rachel was tempted to say something mean to her brother but figured he would say something even meaner.

You're the silly child, she thought as she hurried along. *Someday you'll be sorry you teased me so much, and I hope it's before we're both old and gray.*

When Rachel arrived at school, she spotted several sleds lined up near the porch. Orlie Troyer stood nearby talking with another boy.

"Guder mariye, Rachel," he said. "I see you brought your sled with you today."

"Good morning." Rachel leaned her sled against the building. "I can hardly wait for recess. It will be so much fun to go sledding."

Orlie motioned to his sled. "I'm sure I'll have more

fun than anyone else, since I've got the fastest sled here."

"I'll bet my sled's faster," Rachel said.

Orlie wrinkled his freckled nose. "Bet it's not."

Before Rachel could respond, Orlie said, "How about if I race you at recess and we'll see who has the fastest sled?"

Rachel nodded. "I'd be happy to race you. I was going to suggest that."

Just then their teacher, Elizabeth Miller, rang the school bell. Jacob nudged Rachel's arm. "We'd better get inside."

"Jah, okay." Rachel hurried into the room with the rest of the children who'd been in the snowy schoolyard.

Rachel hung her coat on a wall peg near the door and placed her black outer bonnet and lunch pail on the shelf above. Then she went to her desk.

Elizabeth tapped her desk bell, signaling for everyone to get quiet. "Good morning, boys and girls."

"Good morning, Elizabeth," the children said.

Rachel was happy that Elizabeth was back from her trip to Tennessee. She'd gone there shortly before Christmas to see her grandmother. Rachel had missed Elizabeth.

Elizabeth opened her Bible and read from Proverbs 14:5: "A truthful witness does not deceive, but a false witness pours out lies."

Rachel cringed as she thought about this morning when Mom had wondered how Cuddles had gotten in the house.

As soon as I get home I'd better tell Mom the truth about letting Cuddles into my room last night, Rachel decided.

"*Psst. . .*Rachel, stand for prayer." Mary nudged Rachel's arm from across the aisle.

Rachel jumped to her feet and bowed her head as she and the other children said the Lord's Prayer.

After the prayer, everyone filed to the front of the room and sang one song in English and one in German.

When the children returned to their seats, classes began.

For the next hour, Rachel concentrated on her schoolwork. When it was time for morning recess, Rachel hurried to the back of the room, slipped into her heavy wool cape and black bonnet, and rushed out the door.

"Can I take a quick ride?" Rachel's cousin Mary asked when Rachel grabbed hold of her sled.

Rachel's eyebrows furrowed. "Didn't you bring your sled today?"

Mary shook her head. "One of the runners is wobbly. Papa hasn't fixed it yet."

Rachel stared at her sled. Morning recess wasn't very long. If she let Mary borrow the sled, she might not have enough time to race Orlie. Still, Rachel didn't want to be selfish. "I'll let you use my sled after I race Orlie," she said.

"Please, Rachel." Mary pouted. "I'll just take one quick ride—I promise."

"Maybe Mary would like to race me," Orlie said, pulling his sled beside Rachel's.

Mary shook her head. "I just want a nice ride down the hill. I don't want to race anyone."

"That's okay. It's Rachel I promised to race anyway." Orlie gave Rachel his slanted grin. "We can have our race as soon as Mary brings your sled back up the hill."

Rachel nibbled on her lip. As much as she wanted to race Orlie right now, she wanted to please her cousin, too. Mary was Rachel's best friend, and if she didn't let Mary use the sled, Mary might think Rachel was selfish.

"Okay, Mary," Rachel said. "Just one ride, though. Remember, I'm supposed to race Orlie. He thinks he can beat me."

"Jah, okay." Mary grabbed the rope on Rachel's sled and pulled it to the hill behind the schoolhouse where the others were sledding.

Rachel followed. "Just one turn," she reminded her cousin.

Mary sat on the sled and grabbed the rope attached to the steering handles. "Would you please give me a push, Rachel?"

Rachel placed both hands on Mary's back. "One. . . two. . .three!" She pushed hard, but the sled only moved a few inches.

"Try it again, Rachel!" Mary directed over her shoulder. "You're not pushing hard enough."

Rachel gritted her teeth. "I did push hard. The sled

doesn't want to move."

"If it won't move, then it sure won't beat my sled," Orlie said.

"Maybe some snow is stuck to the runners." Mary climbed off the sled and kicked at a clump of snow underneath the runners. Then she climbed back on. "Let's try it again."

"*Ooph!*" Rachel grunted as she gave Mary another hefty shove. This time the sled glided down the hill, but at a snail's pace.

Orlie snickered and nudged Rachel with his elbow. "You won't beat me on that slow sled!"

Rachel frowned. If her sled wouldn't go any faster than this, how could she beat Orlie?

"I think I'll take my sled for a trial run," Orlie said. "As fast as my sled goes, I should be back up here before Mary makes it to the bottom."

Rachel frowned again. Could Orlie's sled really be that fast?

Orlie jumped on his sled, pushed off with his feet, and—*zip!*—he sailed down the hill so fast it looked like he was flying.

"Oh great," she muttered. "Unless I can figure out some way to make my sled go faster than that, I'll never win a race against Orlie."

"That wasn't much of a ride, was it?" Rachel asked when Mary trudged up the hill several minutes later. Orlie was right behind her, wearing a triumphant smile.

Mary shrugged. "I thought the ride was okay."

"Maybe I need to wax the runners." Rachel wished she'd brought one of Mom's candles from home. Her brother Henry had told her once that candles worked well for waxing sled runners.

Orlie sauntered up to Rachel and shook his head. "Your sled is really slow. Are you sure you want to race me, Rachel?"

"Maybe you shouldn't race Orlie," Mary said. She leaned close to Rachel's ear. "His sled is really fast, and yours goes really slow. I don't see how you can win a race against him."

Rachel patted her cold cheeks to warm them as she pondered the problem. "I'll be right back."

"Where are you going?" Orlie called as Rachel hurried toward the schoolhouse.

She just kept trotting.

Rachel returned several minutes later with a candle she'd borrowed from their teacher. She smiled at Mary. "I'll take my sled now, please."

"What are you planning to do with that candle?" Mary asked.

"You'll see." Rachel squatted beside her sled, flipped it over, and rubbed the candle back and forth across the runners. "That should do the trick!" She turned the sled over again, grabbed the rope, and pulled it to the edge of the hill. "I'm ready when you are, Orlie!"

"Ready as I'll ever be!" Orlie looked at Rachel and

winked. "This will be a piece of cake."

Rachel nodded. "I'm sure it will, only it will be *my* piece of cake."

"We'll see about that," Orlie grunted.

"Want me to say when to start?" Mary asked.

Rachel nodded. So did Orlie. All the other children lined up at the top of the hill to watch.

Mary cupped her hands around her mouth. "Get ready. . . Get set. . . Go!"

Everyone cheered as Rachel and Orlie pushed off with their feet. Orlie's sled whooshed ahead of Rachel's, but Rachel's sled picked up speed as it zoomed down the hill. It went so fast she could barely hold the rope. "Yippee!" she hollered. "I'm going to win this race!"

Whap!—the rope snapped in two. Rachel could no longer control which way she was going. "Oh no!" she cried. Rachel's sled was out of control—she headed straight for the creek!

Chapter 2

A Troublesome Day

Rachel rose out of the water sputtering and mumbling, "Always trouble somewhere."

A hand reached out to Rachel. Orlie stood in the water beside her sled. "What happened, Rachel? Are you okay?"

"I–I'm not hurt. I'm sure I'll be fine once my clothes are dry." Rachel tried to get up on her own, but fell back in the water with a *splash!*

"Here, let me help you," Orlie offered, extending his hand again.

Rachel took Orlie's hand, clambered to her feet, and plodded out of the water, pulling her sled along.

Mary stepped up to Rachel. "You shouldn't have waxed those runners so much. What were you thinking?"

"I thought if I waxed the runners it would make my sled go faster so I could win the race," Rachel explained. "My sled did go faster. If the rope hadn't broken, I would have won."

"Jah, right," Orlie said, shaking his head.

Mary grabbed one end of the broken rope, while Rachel grabbed the other. As they sloshed back up the hill, Rachel grumbled. She didn't like being wet and cold, and she didn't like losing the race. She wished she hadn't raced Orlie at all. She wished it was summer!

When Rachel entered the classroom, Elizabeth exclaimed, "Rachel, your clothes are wet! What happened?"

Rachel explained about the race and the broken rope that caused her to lose control of her sled.

"You shouldn't have waxed those runners," Mary put in.

"I—I know. You s—said that already." Rachel's teeth chattered so much she could barely talk. "If the r—rope hadn't broken, and the cr—creek hadn't b—been in the way, I would have w—won that race."

"You don't always have to win, Rachel," Mary said.

Rachel just rubbed her hands briskly over her cold arms.

"Rachel and Orlie, you both need to stand in front of the woodstove until your clothes are dry," Elizabeth instructed. "Otherwise, you might catch a cold."

"I'm not that wet, Teacher," Orlie said. "Just my boots and the bottom of my pants got wet when I went to help Rachel."

Elizabeth nodded. "Then take off your boots and socks and set them by the stove."

Orlie did as their teacher said then sat at his desk.

"What about my schoolwork?" Rachel asked. "How can I do that if I'm standing in front of the stove?"

"Maybe we could move your desk closer to the stove," Elizabeth suggested.

Rachel opened her mouth to reply, but all that came out was a big *ah-choo!*

Elizabeth's forehead wrinkled. "I think it will take too long for your clothes to dry with you still wearing them. You probably need to go home for the rest of the day."

"What about the spelling test tomorrow?" Spelling was Rachel's best subject, and she didn't want to miss studying for it.

"I'll give you the list of words," Elizabeth said. "You can practice them at home." She motioned to her helper, Sharon Smucker, who was helping the younger children with their coats. "Sharon, would you please get your horse and buggy ready and take Rachel home?"

"Of course I'll take her home." Sharon smiled at Rachel. "I should have the horse and buggy ready to go in a few minutes, so you stay here where it's warm. I'll pull up out front when I'm ready."

"Danki [thank you]." Rachel moved closer to the stove, and Sharon hurried out the door.

When Rachel arrived home from school, she found Mom sitting at the kitchen table, reading the newspaper. The fire in the woodstove crackled and snapped, spilling its warmth into the room.

Mom looked up as Rachel stepped in. "Rachel, what are you doing home from school so soon?" She glanced at the clock on the far wall. "It's not even noon yet."

Rachel explained about the sled going out of control, and how she'd landed in the creek.

Mom squinted. "*Ach* [oh], Rachel, you're right—you are soaking wet!"

Rachel sneezed. "That's why Elizabeth sent me home. She didn't think my clothes would dry fast enough in front of the woodstove at school."

"You could go back to school after you change clothes," Mom suggested, "but I'm worried you might catch a cold."

"Elizabeth said I could stay home the rest of the day." Rachel lifted her backpack. "She gave me a list of spelling words to study."

"That's good," Mom said with a smile. "While you're getting out of those wet clothes, I'll run warm water in the tub so you can take a bath. After you finish your homework, you can help me bake a shoofly pie."

Rachel licked her lips. "Yum." She always enjoyed eating one of Mom's delicious molasses-filled pies.

After Rachel had gone over her spelling lesson, Mom set out a glass pie pan. "After the pie is done, I'll whip some cream, so we can have it with our pie tonight." Her glasses had slipped to the middle of her nose, and she pushed them back in place.

"That sounds *gut* [good]," Rachel said as she put her choring apron over her dress. "Mom, I've been wondering about something."

"What's that?"

"Since your glasses never seem to stay in place, why you don't get some new ones."

"New glasses wouldn't do me any good," Mom said.

"Why not?"

Mom reached under her glasses and rubbed the skinniest part of her nose. "The bridge of my nose is very narrow. I've always had trouble keeping my glasses in place."

Rachel touched the bridge of her own nose and frowned. She hoped she never had to wear glasses.

"Why don't you get out the pie ingredients while I roll the dough?" Mom motioned to the cupboard across the room.

"What do I need?"

"You'll need molasses, baking soda, brown sugar, eggs, and hot water for the filling. For the crumb part, you'll need flour, brown sugar, butter, nutmeg, and cinnamon," Mom said. "Oh, and would you please get some salt? I'll need to fill the salt shaker on the table before we have supper."

Rachel hurried to the cupboard where Mom kept baking supplies. She set out each item while repeating it to Mom so she wouldn't forget anything. She didn't want the shoofly pie to turn out terrible, like the cookies she made last summer when she used baking soda instead of baking powder and didn't put in enough sugar.

Mom watched Rachel measure the ingredients. When the filling and crumbs had been mixed in a bowl and put into the pie shell, Mom smiled at Rachel and said, "It looks like I have enough dough left over for another pie. Why don't you make the second pie? Then you can put both pies in the oven."

"Will you watch me make the second pie?" Rachel asked.

Mom covered her mouth and yawned. "I'm feeling kind of tired, so I thought I'd lie on the sofa a while."

"Are you okay, Mom?"

"I'm fine—just tired," Mom said as she turned on the oven. "I'm sure you'll do okay, but if you need any help, follow the recipe in the cookbook on the counter."

Mom sure is tired a lot lately. I guess it's because she'll soon have a baby. Rachel looked at the pie she'd put together with Mom. *I did all right when Mom was here. I hope I don't mess things up on my own.*

Rachel propped the toe of her right foot on the heel of her left foot as she stared at the ingredients on the counter. "Everything's here. I just need to make sure I put the right amount of each ingredient in the pie."

As Rachel added a cup of molasses to the bowl, she thought about the spelling test they would have at school tomorrow. Even though spelling was her best subject and she'd already read through the list, she wanted to study more so she'd get a perfect score.

She glanced at her backpack, hanging from a wall peg near the back door. Maybe she could study for the spelling test while she made the pie. *Jah, that's just what I'll do!*

Rachel placed her spelling words on the counter next to the cookbook. As she added another ingredient to the bowl, she said the first spelling word: "Celebrate. C-e-l-e-b-r-a-t-e."

She stirred the filling with a wooden spoon as she said the next word. "Mediate. M-e-d-i-t-a-t-e." She shook her head. "No, it's mediate, not meditate. M-e-d-i-a-t-e." Rachel moved to the next word. "Selection. S-e-l-e-c-t-i-o-n. These words are so easy—a piece of cake," she said with a giggle. "No, make that a piece of pie."

Rachel continued to repeat the spelling words as she added the rest of the ingredients and poured half the filling into the pie crust. Next, she sprinkled half the crumb mixture over the filling then added more filling and the rest of the crumbs. Carefully, she carried the pie to the oven and set it on the rack. Then she did the same with the pie she and Mom had made together. She closed the oven door and set the timer for ten minutes.

Rachel grabbed her spelling words and sat at the table. Soon the kitchen was filled with warmth from the stove and a delicious aroma of pies baking in the oven.

Ding! Ding! Ding!—the timer went off. Rachel turned the heat down to 350 degrees and set the timer for fifty more minutes. Rachel set two cooling racks on the counter and went back to the table to study her list of spelling words.

Ding! Ding! Ding!—the timer went off again.

When Rachel opened the oven door this time, the sweet smell of molasses rose with the steam. The edges of both pies were lightly brown—just perfect. She removed the pies and set them on the cooling racks then headed back to the table. If she studied her spelling words until Mom came back to the kitchen, she was sure to get a good grade on the test.

After supper that evening, Mom announced that she and Rachel had made shoofly pie for dessert.

"Yum." Jacob smacked his lips. "Is there any whipping cream to go with it?"

"Jah, there is," Mom said as she set one of the pies on the table. She smiled at Rachel. "I put the second pie shell in an aluminum pan, so this I know is the one you baked yourself. Would you like to cut and serve it for us?"

Rachel nodded, feeling pleased with herself. The pie she had baked looked as good as the one in the glass pan that she'd helped Mom make. She was sure her pie would taste delicious.

Rachel hurried across the room, took out six plates, and placed them on the table—one each for Grandpa Schrock, Pap, Henry, Jacob, Mom, and one for herself. Next, she got out a knife and cut the pie into six hefty pieces. She lifted out the first one and placed it on Grandpa's plate. Since he was the oldest member of their family, she thought he should be the first to taste her delicious pie.

While Rachel was serving the others, Grandpa dipped a spoon into the bowl of whipping cream Mom had set on the table. He winked at Rachel and forked a piece of pie into his mouth. As he began to chew, a strange look came over his face. His bushy gray eyebrows pulled together. His nose twitched. His lips curled up at the corners.

Rachel figured Mom probably hadn't put enough sugar in the whipping cream.

Pap took a bite of his pie and quickly reached for his glass of water.

"This pie sure looks good," Henry said. He took a bite, dashed across the room, and spit the pie into the sink. "Ugh! That tastes *baremlich* [terrible]! What did you do to this pie, Rachel?"

"I—I don't know. I thought I did everything Mom told me to do with the first pie." Rachel's throat felt clogged and tears sprang to her eyes. First the mishap with her sled at school and now a ruined pie! Couldn't she do anything right? This had sure been a troublesome day!

Jacob tasted his pie then, and quickly dumped it in the garbage can. "This is the worst shoofly pie I've ever tasted! It's not even fit for a fly." He squinted at Rachel. "We'll probably all get the fly flu after eating this, and then our faces will turn blue."

"Jacob Yoder, that's a terrible thing to say," Mom said, shaking her head. "I'm sure Rachel didn't ruin the pie." She poked her fork into her piece and took a bite. Her lips curled, the way Grandpa's had, and she reached for her glass of water. "Ach, Rachel, the pie's not sweet enough, and it tastes salty."

Jacob placed his plate in the sink next to Henry's. "Maybe Rachel ruined the pie on purpose so we'd all get the fly flu and our faces would turn blue."

Rachel's chin quivered. *I won't cry in front of Jacob. I won't give him the satisfaction.*

"Stop teasing your sister, Jacob," Pap scolded. "I'm sure you couldn't bake a pie any better than hers."

"Bet I could."

Rachel was on the verge of telling Jacob that he could help Mom do the baking from now on, but Mom spoke first. "How much *melassich* [molasses] did you use, Rachel?"

"One cup," Rachel replied.

"How much brown sugar did you put in the filling?"

"Brown sugar?" Rachel stared at a stain on the tablecloth. "I—uh—think maybe I forgot the brown sugar."

"Did you put brown sugar in the crumb mixture?" Grandpa asked, his bushy gray eyebrows lifting high on his forehead.

Rachel pursed her lips. "I'm not sure. I was studying my spelling words while I mixed the ingredients. That must be why I forgot the brown sugar."

"Did you use any salt?" Mom asked.

Rachel thought hard. "Jah, I think I did. It was sitting on the cupboard, so—"

Mom shook her head as she clucked her tongue. "The recipe I use calls for cinnamon and nutmeg in the crumb mixture, but no salt."

"But a box of salt was on the cupboard," Rachel sputtered.

"I asked you to set that out so I could fill the salt shaker on the table, remember?"

Rachel nodded slowly.

"No wonder Rachel's pie tastes so baremlich," Jacob said when he returned to the table. "Can I have a piece of the pie you made, Mom?"

Mom shook her head. "Not until you apologize to your sister for saying her pie is baremlich."

"But it is terrible," Jacob insisted. "In fact, it's the worst shoofly pie I've ever tasted!"

Rachel couldn't stand anymore. Sniffling, she ran out of the kitchen and up the stairs two at a time. She flew into her room and flopped onto her bed. She lay there staring at the ceiling. "I am a little bensel!"

A few minutes later, the door creaked open, and Mom stepped into the room. She sat beside Rachel and took her hand. "A ruined pie isn't the end of the world."

"Jacob and Henry think it is. They always make fun of me when I mess up." *Sniff! Sniff!* "I can never do anything right."

"That's not true." Mom pointed across the room to the collection of rocks Rachel had painted. "You made those look like ladybugs and turtles. Not everyone can paint as well as you do, daughter."

Rachel swiped at the tears rolling down her cheeks. "I thought I might try painting a rock to look like Cuddles sometime."

"That's a fine idea," Mom said with a nod.

Rachel remembered that she hadn't told Mom the truth about the cat in the house last night. She swallowed hard and sat up. "I—I need to tell you something, Mom."

"What's that?"

"When Cuddles bumped into the dustpan this morning, and you said you wondered how she'd gotten inside, I should have told you the truth."

"What truth?"

"I heard scratching at my window last night. When I opened it, Cuddles was in the tree, begging to get in." Rachel drew in a quick breath. "The wind was howling, and it was cold out there in the snow, so I—"

"Let the cat come into your room," Mom said, finishing Rachel's sentence.

Rachel nodded.

"Was Cuddles on your bed?"

"Jah."

"You know I don't mind the cat being inside as long as she's wearing a flea collar, but I don't approve of her being on your bed."

"I'm sorry for letting Cuddles sleep on my bed," Rachel said. "And I'm sorrier for not telling you sooner."

Mom gave Rachel a hug. "I accept your apology, and I'm glad you told the truth. Confession's always good for the soul."

Rachel nodded and nestled against Mom's chest. At least the troublesome day had ended on a good note.

Chapter 3

True or False

Wheeee!" Rachel stretched out her legs as she hung onto the rope dangling from the hayloft in their barn. "This is fun!" she shouted to Jacob, who was cleaning one of the horse stalls. "Do you want to take a turn?"

Jacob held up the shovel in his hands. "I'd like to, but I've got work to do." He squinted at Rachel. "If I'm not mistaken, you're supposed to be in the house, studying for tomorrow's history test."

Rachel let go of the rope and dropped into the mound of hay below. "I'll study later. Right now I think I'll visit old Tom," she said, scrambling to her feet.

Jacob frowned. "You'll be sorry if you flunk that test."

"I passed my spelling test last week."

"That's different; you like spelling."

It was true—spelling came easy to Rachel. History was harder for her, and she didn't enjoy it nearly as much as she did spelling.

"I'll study later." Rachel headed for the stall where

Pap's old buggy horse was kept when he wasn't in the pasture. Old Tom couldn't pull their buggy anymore, so Rachel visited him as often as she could.

As Rachel stepped into Tom's stall, the sweet smell of fresh hay tickled her nose.

She was glad Tom had a nice warm place to stay during the cold winter months. She was glad Pap had kept the horse even though he was getting old and couldn't do much.

"How are you doing, Tom?"

Tom dropped his head, and Rachel stroked his silky brown mane. "Are you warm enough here in the barn?"

Tom whinnied and nuzzled Rachel's hand with his warm nose.

"Sorry, but I didn't bring you a treat today," Rachel said. "If Mom has any apples, I'll bring you one tomorrow."

Tom lifted his head and snorted. He moved away from Rachel and found a spot to lie down in the hay.

Rachel figured Tom wanted to take a nap, so she left the stall and went to look for a ball of string, hoping to play with Cuddles. She found some string on a shelf where Pap kept his tools. She hurried toward a pile of straw on the other side of the barn, where Cuddles liked to sleep.

"What are you up to now?" Jacob asked as Rachel passed him.

"I'm going to play with Cuddles."

"I thought you were gonna study for the history test."

"You're not my boss," she mumbled. "I said I would study later."

Who did Jacob think he was, trying to tell her what to do?

"Never said I was." Jacob leaned the shovel against the wall. "I'm done cleaning, so I'm gonna do my homework. Are you sure you don't want to do yours now, too?"

She shook her head. "I can study after supper."

"Suit yourself." Jacob shrugged and headed out the door.

Rachel hurried over to the pile of straw, but Cuddles wasn't there. "Where are you, Cuddles? Come, kitty, kitty," she called.

She spotted Cuddles in the far corner of the barn, chasing a tiny gray mouse. "Stop it!" she scolded. "Leave that poor *maus* [mouse] alone."

Cuddles paid no attention to Rachel and continued the chase. Round and round the barn she went—leaping in the air, swiping with her paws, and meowing for all she was worth.

Rachel hollered for Cuddles to stop, but her yelling made no difference. "If you hurt that maus, you'll get no supper tonight." She shook her finger as the cat and mouse whizzed past again. "I won't let you chase my bubbles anymore!"

The mouse darted into a hole near one of the cow's stalls. Cuddles slammed into the wall. *Meow!* She shook her furry head and looked up at Rachel as if to say,

"Don't you feel sorry for me?"

Rachel clucked her tongue, the way Mom often did. "That wouldn't have happened if you had listened to me."

Cuddles swiped a paw across Rachel's shoe. *Meow! Meow!*

Rachel thought about how sad she felt whenever she got in trouble. Maybe Cuddles felt that way, too. She bent down and scooped the cat into her arms. "I love you, Cuddles, but you must learn to listen."

Cuddles responded with a sandpapery kiss on Rachel's chin and began to purr.

Rachel found a seat on a bale of straw and placed Cuddles on her lap. It felt nice to sit in the warm barn and stroke her silky cat. It was a lot more fun than sitting at the kitchen table, studying for a history test she didn't want to take.

Rachel leaned her head against the wall and closed her eyes. *It's supposed to be a true or false test, so it might not be too hard. Maybe I can guess at which answers are right and which are wrong.*

During supper that evening, Rachel told her family about Cuddles and the mouse. "I hollered at Cuddles," she said, reaching for a pickle, "but the cat kept chasing that poor little maus."

"There are some things we just can't control," Grandpa said. "Stopping a cat from chasing a mouse is one of those things."

"That's right," Pap said with a nod. "Cuddles was doing what comes naturally for a cat, and it wasn't something you could control."

Rachel bit into the pickle and puckered her lips. She loved dill pickles, even if they were a bit tangy.

"Did you get all your homework done?" Mom asked, turning to Rachel.

Rachel opened her mouth to reply, but Jacob spoke first. "She never even opened her books." He stared at Rachel. "All she's done since she got home from school is play in the barn, dangle from the rope, pet Old Tom, and chase Cuddles."

Pap's eyebrows drew together as he frowned at Rachel. "Don't you have a history test in the morning?"

"Jah. I'll study after supper," she said.

Pap nodded and reached for the platter of roast beef. "I hope you do well on the test."

Rachel hoped that, too.

When supper was over and the dishes were done, Rachel headed for the stairs leading to her room.

"Don't forget your schoolbooks," Mom called. "You left them on the counter near the back door."

Rachel turned back and scooped up the books. When she entered her room, she placed the books on her dresser and sat on the end of her bed. *Brrr.* She rubbed her hands briskly over her arms. "It sure is cold up here."

She reached for the extra quilt at the foot of her bed and wrapped it around her shoulders. Then she moved to the window and lifted the shade. The moon shone brightly, making the snow-covered yard glisten like a blanket of twinkling fireflies. It was a perfect night for sledding.

Rachel shivered as she thought about her recent sledding experience when she ended up in the creek. She would have to be more careful the next time she took her sled to school.

She leaned close to the frosty window and blew on it. A circle formed on the glass where her hot breath made contact. Using her finger, she drew her name. She blew again, and the clock by her bed kept time with her breathing. *Tick-tock. Tick-tock. Breathe in. . .blow out.*

Rachel stretched her arms over her head and yawned. She felt so sleepy. Maybe she would stretch out on the bed and rest awhile before she studied.

Cock-a-doodle-do! Cock-a-doodle-do!

Rachel sat up with a start. Was that the rooster crowing? Their old red rooster had never crowed in the middle of the night before.

She rolled over and stared at the clock by her bed. It was 6 a.m.!

Rachel glanced down at her wrinkled dress and gasped. *I must have fallen asleep last night and never got ready for bed!*

She scrambled out of bed and hurried to her dresser. When she opened a drawer and took out a pair of clean socks, she spotted her schoolbooks on top of the dresser. "Oh no! I didn't study for the history test!"

Rachel glanced at the clock. It was too late to study now. She needed to get washed, dressed, and hurry downstairs to help Mom with breakfast. *Maybe I can study on the way to school. Jah, that's what I'll do.*

As Rachel trudged through the slippery snow toward the schoolhouse, she found it hard to hold her history book, which she had taken out of her backpack. Each time she took a step, the book shifted in her hands.

"Always trouble somewhere," Rachel grumbled as the book snapped shut.

"If you weren't trying to study while you walk, you wouldn't have so much trouble." Jacob snickered. "My silly *schweschder* [sister], the little bensel."

Rachel glared at Jacob. "I am not a silly child!"

"Jah, you are."

"Am not."

"Are so."

And so it went until Rachel and Jacob reached the schoolhouse. Between trying to keep her history book open and arguing with Jacob, Rachel hadn't studied at all. If she didn't think of some way to control this situation, she would probably fail her history test.

Rachel stomped the snow off her boots and was about to enter the schoolhouse when someone tapped her shoulder. She whirled around. There stood freckle-faced Orlie, wearing his usual crooked grin.

"Are you ready for another sled race during recess?" he asked.

Rachel shook her head. "I didn't bring my sled with me today."

"Maybe you can borrow your cousin Mary's sled." Orlie nudged Rachel's arm. "Mary said her daed fixed her wobbly runner last night, so she brought the sled with her today."

"No thanks. I'm not interested in racing you again."

"You don't feel like taking another swim in the creek, huh?"

Rachel ground her teeth together. Orlie teased as much as Jacob. Did he enjoy making fun of her?

She pushed past Orlie and stepped into the schoolhouse, where a burst of toasty air greeted her. Elizabeth had stoked the woodstove so the scholars would be warm and snug.

Rachel hoped to have time to study for the history test during the morning, but Elizabeth kept everyone busy with arithmetic problems.

Rachel had a hard time concentrating on arithmetic when she only wanted to open her history book and study for the test they'd take after their noon recess.

When Elizabeth announced that it was time for morning recess, Rachel thought she might have time to look at her history book. But Mary insisted that Rachel join her and the other girls in a snowball fight against the boys.

"Oh, all right," Rachel finally agreed. She didn't want to disappoint Mary.

Everyone put on their coats, gloves, and hats, and hurried outside.

"Let's wait until each team has one hundred snowballs made before we start," Phoebe Byler suggested.

Aaron King grunted. "If we took the time to make that many snowballs, recess would be over before the snowball fight began."

"Aaron's right," Orlie put in. "Let's have each girl make three snowballs, and each boy make five snowballs."

"That's not right," Rachel spoke up. "Why should the boys get to make more snowballs than the girls?"

"Because there are eighteen girls and only twelve boys." Orlie planted his hands on his hips like he was the boss. "That will give the girls fifty-four snowballs and the boys will have—"

"Sixty!" Mary shouted. "That's not right!"

Jacob stepped forward. "Jah, it is. Since there are fewer boys than girls, we need an advantage."

"No, you don't," Becky Esh said with a shake of her head.

"Do so." Orlie insisted.

"Do not."

"Do so."

"Do not."

Rachel threw a snowball. *Splat!* It hit Orlie's cheek and ran down his neck.

"Hey, that was not fair! I wasn't ready!" He bent down, scooped a handful of snow, and threw it at Rachel.

She ducked, and the snowball whizzed over her head. "Ha! You missed me!" she shouted as she ran away.

Orlie chased Rachel, and everyone started making snowballs fast and flinging them at whoever got in their way. So much for a snowball fight with the girls against the boys!

Soon Elizabeth called to the children. A group of laughing red-nosed, rosy-cheeked scholars returned to the schoolhouse and hung up their coats, hats, and gloves. After everyone was seated at their desks, the curtain dividing the room was drawn, and grades three through eight were given a reading lesson, followed by a time of questions from the teacher about what they had learned.

At eleven thirty, the children were dismissed by rows to wash their hands, get their lunch boxes, and return to their seats. It was too cold to eat outside like they did on warmer days. After eating their lunches, the children were allowed to play outside until twelve thirty.

I have plenty of time to study for the test now, Rachel thought as the other children donned their coats and filed out the door.

Rachel remained in her seat. She was reaching for her history book when Elizabeth asked, "Aren't you going outside to play with the others?"

"Not this time." Rachel shook her head. "It's too cold out, and I thought I would—"

"If you're not going outside, would you like to help me cut out some paper stars?"

"What are they for?" Rachel asked.

"Each time someone gets a perfect score on a lesson, he or she will get to pick out a star and write his or her name on it," Elizabeth replied. "A perfect score on a test will get the scholar two paper stars."

"Oh, I see."

"We'll put the stars around the schoolhouse and see if we can get so many that they go up to the ceiling." Elizabeth patted Rachel's head. "If you and I get some stars cut out now, we'll have enough to give everyone who gets a perfect score on the history test this afternoon."

Rachel knew if she spent the next half hour cutting out paper stars, she would have no time to study for the test. She couldn't tell Elizabeth she didn't want to help because she hadn't studied.

"Won't Sharon help you with the stars?" Rachel asked.

Elizabeth shook her head. "I asked her to go outside with the scholars." She frowned. "After the snowball fight during morning recess, I figured either Sharon or I should be outside to be sure everything goes well."

Forcing a smile, Rachel nodded and said, "Okay, I'll

help you cut out the stars."

Elizabeth gave Rachel a stack of colored paper, a pattern to trace the stars, and a pair of scissors; then she returned to her own desk and cut out stars, too.

Rachel hummed as she traced the first star onto a sheet of bright yellow paper. This was a lot more fun than studying for the history test would have been.

Lunch recess was over sooner than Rachel had hoped, and when everyone took their seats, Elizabeth said it was time for the middle-grade scholars to take their history test.

As Rachel stared at the true and false questions on the paper she'd been given, a knot formed in her stomach. She didn't know any of the answers. She could only guess.

What if my guesses are wrong? she fretted. *How can I face Mom and Pap if I fail this test?*

Rachel tapped her pencil along the edge of her desk. *Tap-tappety-tap-tap.*

She set the pencil down and placed her arms on top of the desk. Still, no answers came. She looked at the front of the room and stared at the letters and numbers on a wide strip of paper above the blackboard. *Think, Rachel. . .think hard. True or false? False or true?*

Suddenly, an idea popped into Rachel's head. She knew how she might be able to pass the test!

Orlie's desk used to be behind Rachel's, but last week Elizabeth had moved him in front of Rachel, because he kept whispering and tapping Rachel's shoulder. If Rachel craned her neck a bit, she had the perfect view of Orlie's desk.

In that moment, Rachel made a hasty decision. She would copy the answers from Orlie's paper.

Chapter 4

Buddy

Rachel Yoder, I'd like to speak to you," Elizabeth said when class was over for the day. "Orlie Troyer. . .I need to see you as well."

Rachel glanced over her shoulder. Everyone but Jacob had put on his or her coat and was heading out the door. Jacob stood at the back of the room with his arms folded and a scowl on his face.

"Jacob, you may wait outside for your sister." Elizabeth motioned Rachel and Orlie to the front of the room. "*Kumme* [come] now."

Rachel's heart hammered as she shuffled behind Orlie to their teacher's desk. The frown on Elizabeth's face let Rachel know that she'd probably done something wrong.

"I've been going over the true and false answers you both gave on the history test. Neither of you will get a star, because almost every one of your answers was wrong." Elizabeth paused and pointed to the stack of papers on her desk. "The strange thing is that each of you had exactly the same answers." She looked at Orlie. She looked at Rachel. "Which of you copied from the other person's paper?"

Rachel lowered her gaze and scuffed the toe of her shoe against the wooden floor.

"I don't know what you're talking about, Teacher," Orlie said. "I never copied anyone's paper."

Elizabeth touched Rachel's arm. "True or false, Rachel? Did you copy Orlie's paper?"

Rachel forced herself to look at the teacher. "True."

Elizabeth's forehead wrinkled. "Why would you do something like that?"

"I—I didn't know the answers," Rachel mumbled. "I was afraid to guess."

"You shouldn't have had to guess. Didn't you study?" Elizabeth questioned.

Rachel slowly shook her head. "I was going to study last night, but I fell asleep on my bed with my clothes on and didn't wake up until this morning." She drew in a quick breath. "I tried to study on the way to school, but my history book kept flopping shut. I figured I could study during morning recess, but Mary wanted me to join her and the others in the snow. Then after lunch, you asked me to cut out the stars, so—"

"No excuses, Rachel. I'm sure you could have made time to study yesterday if you'd wanted to." Elizabeth looked over at Orlie. "What about you? How much did you study for the test?"

Orlie's face turned red as a radish. "I tried to study, but I felt so bad when my *mamm* [mom] said I'd have to get rid of Buddy that I couldn't think about anything else."

"Who's Buddy?" Rachel asked, hoping the change of subject might take Elizabeth's mind off the history test.

"Buddy's my dog. Mama's been havin' sneezing fits lately and the doctor thinks she's allergic to Buddy." Orlie blinked his eyes and sniffed a couple of times. "Last night my daed said I'd have to find Buddy a new home."

"I'm sorry about that," Elizabeth said, "but it doesn't excuse you from studying." She leveled Rachel with a serious look. "And there's no excuse for cheating!"

Rachel cringed. When she'd copied Orlie's answers, she knew it was wrong. But she did it anyway. "I–I'm sorry, Teacher. I promise I'll never cheat on another test."

"I certainly hope not." Elizabeth motioned to Orlie. "Don't you think you owe him an apology, too?"

Rachel turned to face Orlie. "I'm sorry for copying your paper."

Elizabeth glanced out the window. "It's beginning to snow pretty hard, so you'd both better go home. For the rest of this week, Rachel will stay after school for one hour and do extra work." She reached for a sheet of paper, scribbled a note, and handed it to Rachel. "This is for your parents, letting them know that you cheated on the history test and what your punishment will be here at school."

Rachel swallowed hard. No doubt she would be punished at home, too.

"Are you gonna punish me, Teacher?" Orlie asked.

Elizabeth shook her head. "You didn't cheat, but you do need to study when you have a test."

He nodded. "From now on, I will."

"That will be all," Elizabeth said. "I'll see you both in the morning."

Rachel shuffled toward the door.

"Say, Rachel," Orlie said, as he, Jacob, and Rachel left the schoolyard together, "would you like to have a big shaggy dog named Buddy?"

"No thanks," she said with a shake of her head. "All the big shaggy dogs I've met like to bark and jump up on people."

"Buddy doesn't bark much," Orlie said. "And he only jumps up when he gets excited."

"No thanks," Rachel said again. "I've got a cat. Cats and dogs don't get along very well."

"They can learn to get along, just like people." Orlie stepped in front of Rachel. "Please say you'll take Buddy. I need to find him a good home."

"Sorry, but it won't be at *our* home." Rachel pushed past Orlie. She used to think Orlie was her friend, but why would a friend try to shove his mutt off onto someone who didn't want a dog?

"I'll take him," Jacob announced. "I asked for a puppy for my birthday a few years ago, but Mom said no to that because puppies make too many messes." His face broke into a wide smile. "Since Buddy's a full-grown dog, I don't think Mom will mind!"

"Well, I mind." Rachel's eyes narrowed. "Cuddles wouldn't like to have a big dog chasing her all the time."

"I'll train him to not chase the cat," Jacob said.

"How will you do that?"

Jacob shrugged. "I'll figure out something."

"Why don't you stop by my house on your way home?" Orlie suggested. "Then you can meet Buddy and decide if you'd like to take him home."

"No!" Rachel shouted.

"Yes!" Jacob hollered. "Orlie's place is right on the way, so we'll stop there now and meet Buddy."

When they arrived at Orlie's place, Rachel spotted Orlie's little sisters playing in the snow. She was tempted to join them, but Orlie nudged her arm and said, "Buddy's probably in the barn. I'll get him."

A few minutes later, Orlie returned from the barn with a big, red, shaggy dog.

Woof! The dog wagged his tail, jumped up, and licked Rachel's face.

"Ha ha! He likes you," Jacob said with a chuckle.

"Ha ha, yourself." Rachel wrinkled her nose and crossed her eyes at Jacob. Then she pushed the dog away.

"Come on, Rachel. Don't give me that look. You know you like Buddy."

"I do not like him. He's big and hairy, and his tongue's wet and slimy!"

Orlie patted the dog's head. "He was only trying to be friendly." He looked at Jacob with a hopeful expression. "Do you like him?"

"Oh jah, I sure do!" Jacob said with a vigorous nod.

"Then why don't you take him home and see if your folks will let you keep him?"

"No!" Rachel shouted.

"Yes!" Jacob hollered.

"Danki," said Orlie. "It will make me feel much better if Buddy has a good home."

"Mom and Pap haven't said you could keep him yet," Rachel reminded her brother.

"I know," Jacob said, "but I'm hoping they'll say yes when they see how *wunderbaar* [wonderful] he is."

"I don't think he's wonderful, and I'm hoping they say no," Rachel mumbled.

"I'll get Buddy's leash so you can walk him home." Orlie dashed back to the barn. When he returned, he clipped a brown leather leash to Buddy's collar and patted the dog's head. "Good-bye, boy. Be good for Jacob. I'll come see you whenever I can."

Woof! Buddy wagged his tail and licked Orlie's hand.

"I guess we'd better go," Jacob said.

Rachel and Jacob had just started walking down the

driveway when Orlie called, "Wait! I forgot to give you something!" He dashed to Jacob, reached into his pants pocket, and pulled out a plastic whistle. "Here, this is for you!"

"What's it for?" Jacob questioned.

"I trained Buddy with it. He comes when I blow it." Orlie placed the whistle in Jacob's hand. "It will also make him stop if he's running away from you."

"Danki, Orlie." Jacob smiled and put the whistle in his jacket pocket.

"You're welcome."

"See you at school." Jacob started walking again, with Buddy plodding beside him on the leash. Rachel walked on the other side of Jacob, wishing she could say something to make Jacob give up on the idea of taking Buddy home.

"See how nicely Buddy walks for me?" Jacob said. "I think he and I are gonna be real good friends. He seems to like you, too, Rachel."

Rachel only shrugged as Buddy nudged her hand with his cold nose. She trudged through the snow, gritting her teeth. Not only did she have a note in her backpack letting Mom and Pap know she'd been caught cheating, but a gross dog would probably live at their place from now on!

When Rachel and Jacob entered their yard, Jacob took Buddy to the barn. "I don't want him running back to

Orlie's before I talk to Mom and Pap about letting me keep him," Jacob said to Rachel. "Don't say anything to Mom until I've talked to Pap," he added.

Rachel just grunted and headed for the house. She found Mom in the kitchen, baking chocolate chip cookies. They sure smelled good, but Rachel knew she wouldn't be able to eat any until she confessed that she cheated on the history test and had given Elizabeth's note to Mom.

"Hello, Rachel," Mom said as she put a tray of cookies into the oven. "Are you late getting home from school because of the snow?"

"Not really." Rachel dropped her backpack to the floor, slipped out of her coat and bonnet, and hung them on a wall peg near the back door. Then she picked up the backpack and walked across the room. "I did something today that I'm ashamed of," she said, sitting at the table.

Mom turned and wiped her floury hands on her apron. "What was that?"

"I—I cheated on my history test, and here's a note from Elizabeth." Rachel reached into her backpack, retrieved the note, and placed it on the table.

Mom sat across from Rachel and picked up the note. "Hmm. . .I see." She squinted and pushed her glasses to the bridge of her nose.

"Am I going to get a *bletsching* [spanking]?" Rachel asked.

"No," Mom said. "A spanking would be over with

quickly and soon forgotten."

Rachel breathed a sigh of relief. Maybe she wouldn't be punished. Maybe Mom would just give her a lecture or quote a few scriptures from the Bible about cheating.

Mom dropped the note to the table and stared at Rachel. "Besides staying after school for the next week, when you come home you will have no playtime, and you'll do extra chores and studying."

"But, Mom," Rachel argued, "I'll be studying at school, and I already have so many chores."

"Then you shall have a few more." Mom pursed her lips and gave Rachel her "I mean what I say" look. "What you did was wrong. You need to learn a lesson."

"I know it was wrong to cheat, and I promised Elizabeth I would never do it again."

"Even so," Mom said, "You will be punished."

"What about Jacob?" Rachel asked. "Shouldn't he be punished for bringing home a big hairy mutt without asking?"

Mom's eyebrows squeezed together, making a deep wrinkle above her nose. "What are you talking about, Rachel?"

"Orlie Troyer's mutt. Orlie can't keep the dog anymore." Rachel could see by Mom's bewildered expression that she didn't quite believe her. "It's true. Jacob's in the barn right now with Buddy."

"Buddy?"

"Orlie's dog."

Mom stood and pushed back her chair with such force that it toppled. Without bothering to pick it up, she grabbed her shawl off the wall peg and rushed out the door. Rachel followed.

They found Jacob in the barn, kneeling next to Buddy. Jacob jumped up. "I was going to find Pap soon, and then after I spoke with him, I was going to see if you—"

"I already know about the dog," Mom interrupted.

Jacob glared at Rachel. "You weren't supposed to tell. You're nothing but a *retschbeddi* [tattletale]."

"I never promised not to tell Mom." Rachel wrinkled her nose. "And I'm not a tattletale!"

"Jah, you are."

"No, I'm—"

"That will be enough, you two." Mom planted both hands on her hips. "Jacob, why did you bring the dog home without our permission?"

Jacob's chin quivered, and Rachel wondered if he might cry. "Orlie's mamm is allergic to the dog, and Orlie needs to find him a good home. I thought if I brought Buddy home, and you and Pap saw how nice he was, you'd let me keep him."

Mom's expression softened some, as she knelt beside Jacob and stroked Buddy's floppy ear. "He does seem to be a nice *hund* [dog]."

Jacob nodded. "Oh jah, I think he's a wunderbaar hund."

"Even so, you should have asked before you brought

the dog home," Mom said.

Jacob hung his head. "Sorry."

"I didn't want you to have a puppy before because they make so many messes, but since Buddy's a grown dog, puppy messes won't be a problem." Mom touched Jacob's shoulder. "If it's all right with your daed, you can keep the big fluffy dog."

Rachel flopped onto a bale of straw. "No, no," she moaned. She figured Mom had only given in to Jacob's request because he looked like he might cry.

"What's the matter with you, Rachel?" Mom asked. "You have a cat. Why shouldn't Jacob have a pet, too?"

"Because Buddy will chase Cuddles, and he might hurt her."

"He won't," Jacob insisted. "I'll teach him to get along with the cat."

"Humph!" Rachel frowned. "You can't make Buddy be nice to Cuddles any more than I can make Cuddles stop chasing mice."

"I'll bet I can. Buddy's real *schmaert* [smart]. I know he can be trained."

"I don't care how smart he is. He's a dog, and dogs don't like cats!"

Mom stepped between Rachel and Jacob. "Let's end this discussion and wait and see what your daed says about you keeping Buddy."

"Where is Pap? He's not in the barn," Jacob said. "Is he in the house?"

Mom shook her head. "He, Grandpa, and Henry went to town. They said they'd be back in time for supper, but it's probably taking them longer because of the snow. I'm sure they'll be here soon, though."

Rachel squeezed her eyes shut. *I hope when Pap gets home he tells Jacob he can't keep Buddy.*

Chapter 5

More Troubles

For the rest of that week, Rachel had to stay after school every day. She cleaned the blackboards, swept the floor, and did extra reading from her history book. Knowing she had more studying and chores waiting at home made her feel cranky. The only good thing about staying after school was that Henry would pick her up every day with his horse and buggy. Since Jacob had chores to do at home, Mom didn't think it was fair to ask him to wait around the schoolyard until Rachel was ready to go home. Rachel liked that arrangement. Riding in the buggy was warmer than trudging through the cold snow. Besides, she didn't have to put up with Jacob's teasing.

"Are you glad the school week is over?" Henry asked on Friday afternoon when Rachel climbed into his buggy.

She nodded. "I'm happy the weekend is finally here. At least I won't have any more school chores or lessons at the schoolhouse."

"You'll still have chores at home," Henry reminded her.

"Jah, I know—every day but Sunday." Sundays were for rest. All Rachel had to do on Sunday was help Mom serve a light breakfast and get ready for church. This Sunday, church would be held in the main section of Pap's barn. That meant they didn't have to travel to someone else's house for the service.

"From the looks of that sky, I'm guessing we might get more snow," Henry commented as he directed his horse onto the main road.

Rachel looked at the cloudy gray sky. "Maybe it will snow so hard the school board will decide to close the schoolhouse on Monday."

"The weather would have to get pretty bad before they did that." Henry snapped the reins to get his horse, Thunder, moving faster. Thunder turned his head and blew a puff of steam from his mouth. "Besides, think how bored you would be if you had to stay in the house all day."

"I would think of something fun to do," Rachel replied.

"More than likely Mom would think up something for you to do, and it would probably involve work."

Rachel didn't reply. She'd done so many chores this week, she didn't even want to think about work.

When Henry guided his horse and buggy up their driveway, Rachel jumped down. She spotted Cuddles sitting on the porch railing. Had the cat been watching for Rachel? Or maybe she was looking for a mouse.

Rachel sloshed through the snow and stepped onto the porch. She dropped her schoolbooks onto the small table near the door and lifted the cat into her arms. "Did you miss me while I was at school?"

The cat purred and nuzzled Rachel's neck with her cold nose.

"I thought so. I missed you, too, Cuddles."

Rachel was about to bring Cuddles into the house when a furry red blob streaked across the porch. Cuddles hissed and jumped out of Rachel's arms. *Meow!*—she leaped off the porch!

Jacob's dog was right behind Cuddles, barking and swiping the poor cat's tail with his big pink tongue. Rachel wished Pap had said no when Jacob asked if he could keep Buddy. But Pap had seemed almost as eager to have the dog as Jacob had been.

"Halt ei, sell geht zu weit! [Stop, that's going too far!]" Rachel shouted. Where was Jacob, so he could blow that whistle? "Leave my cat alone, you big hairy mutt! Pick on someone your own size!"

Buddy skidded to a stop, whipped around, and raced back to the porch. Cuddles made a beeline for the barn. Rachel released a sigh of relief.

"You're a bad dog," Rachel said, shaking her finger at Buddy.

Slurp! Buddy swiped his tongue across Rachel's finger.

"Yuck! Why do you always lick me?" she grumbled.

Woof! Buddy wagged his tail, tipped his head to one side, and grabbed Rachel's history book in his slobbery mouth. Before Rachel could say a word, Buddy bounded off the porch and headed for the barn.

"Come back here you furry hund!" Rachel slid through the icy snow all the way to the barn. Just inside the door, she spotted Buddy scratching at a pile of straw. She looked around. There was no sign of Cuddles.

Rachel hurried over to Buddy. "What are you up to?"

Woof!

"Did you bury my book in the straw?"

Buddy cocked his head. *Woof! Woof!*

Rachel grunted. "Get out of my way!"

Buddy jumped up, put his huge paws on Rachel's chest, and swiped his slimy tongue across her cheek.

Rachel wrinkled her nose. "*Eww. . .*I think you need a minty doggie bone, because you have bad breath!" She pushed Buddy down with her knee then headed for the pile of straw to look for her book.

Buddy bounded over to Rachel and positioned his bulky body between her and the straw.

"You'd better move," Rachel threatened.

Buddy didn't budge. He just stood there with his tail waging and his tongue hanging out of his mouth.

"I'm warning you. . ."

Woof! Woof! Woof!

"What's the problem?" Henry asked, as he popped

his head over one of the horse's stalls to look at Rachel.

She pointed at Buddy. "*He's* the problem!"

"What's Jacob's dog done now?"

"He chased my cat, stole my history book, and licked my face with his germy tongue." Rachel motioned to the pile of straw behind Buddy. "I think he buried the book in there."

Henry left the stall and grabbed Buddy's collar. "I'll hold the dog while you search for your book."

Rachel knelt in front of the straw and felt all around. "Here it is!" She withdrew the book, dusted it off with her hand, and turned it over. "There are no teeth marks." She glared at Buddy. "It's lucky for you that my book's not ruined."

"I'm glad you found it," Henry said. "I'll put Buddy back in his stall so he won't cause you anymore trouble."

"Good idea." Rachel scrambled to her feet. She was almost to the door when she whirled around. "If you see Jacob, would you give him a message?"

"Jah, sure. What would you like me to tell him?"

"Tell him he'd better keep his promise and teach his dog to be nice to my cat!"

The following day when Rachel entered the barn, she was pleased to discover that the bales of hay that usually sat there had been removed. The floor was clean, too. It was ready for the backless wooden benches they would use for church tomorrow. She noticed that the benches were stacked along one wall. They would probably be set in place sometime later today. In the meantime, Rachel thought the barn was the perfect place to skateboard.

She glanced around. She saw no sign of Cuddles. No sign of Buddy, either. He must be in the empty horse stall where Jacob put him during the night.

Rachel cupped her hands around her mouth and called, "Here, Cuddles! Come kitty, kitty!"

All Rachel heard was the soft nicker of the buggy horses in their stalls at the other end of the barn.

"Cuddles! Where are you, Cuddles?" Rachel moved slowly around the barn, looking in every nook and cranny.

She was ready to give up and return to the house when she heard a faint, *meow.*

Rachel tipped her head and listened.

Meow! Meow! The sound grew louder.

Rachel followed the meowing sound, until she came to the ladder leading to the hayloft. She looked up. Cuddles sat in the hayloft, staring down at her.

Meow!

Rachel clapped her hands. "Here, kitty, kitty."

Cuddles didn't budge.

Rachel started up the ladder. "What a boppli you are, Cuddles." As she picked up Cuddles, the cat dug her claws into Rachel's jacket and meowed louder.

"You're okay," Rachel whispered. "We're almost down."

When Rachel stepped off the ladder, she placed

Cuddles on the floor and hurried to the shelf where she kept her skateboard. When she returned, Cuddles was lying on a straw bale, licking her paws.

Rachel picked up the cat and stepped onto the skateboard, holding Cuddles against her chest. "Here we go, now. This will be fun."

She pushed off with one foot, and the skateboard glided across the barn. She was about to turn and start for the other side of the barn, when Jacob's dog bounded in—*Woof! Woof!* Cuddles shrieked and tried to wriggle free, but Rachel held on tightly.

Woof! Buddy's tail flipped the hem of Rachel's long dress. With another loud bark, Buddy jumped up and swiped his big red tongue across Cuddles's head.

Yeow! Cuddles stuck out her claws and scratched Buddy's nose.

Woof! Woof! Buddy barked, and Cuddles leaped into the air. The skateboard wobbled, and Rachel toppled to the floor. "Trouble seems to follow everywhere I go," she muttered as she clambered to her feet.

Yeow!

Woof!

Rachel turned in time to see Cuddles race out through the barn door with Buddy right behind her. Rachel rushed after them, hollering and waving her arms.

Cuddles and Buddy darted across the yard, zipped around trees, leaped over piles of snow, and slid across the icy lawn.

"Come back here, you two!" Rachel shouted. "Enough is enough!"

Cuddles's hair stood on the back of her neck. Buddy's tail swished. They both kept running.

Since Jacob wasn't there to blow the whistle Orlie had given him, Rachel knew she must do something to stop Jacob's dog from chasing her cat. Cuddles might get hurt!

When the animals raced past again, Rachel grabbed Buddy's collar. Cuddles meowed and leaped over the fence. Buddy let out a howl and tore across the yard, dragging Rachel facedown in the snow.

Jacob stepped into the yard, "Stop, Buddy! Stop!" He skidded across the yard and helped Rachel to her feet. "Are you all right? Why were you hanging onto Buddy's collar?"

"I was trying to save my cat!"

Jacob shook his head. "Don't you think you're overreacting? Buddy may like to chase Cuddles, but he hasn't hurt her, has he?"

"Well, no, but—"

"I think he only chases her because he wants to play."

"I don't think so." Rachel swiped her hand across her face, sending powdery snow all over Jacob.

He jumped back. "Watch what you're doing! I had a bath last night; I don't need a snow shower today!"

"Very funny." Rachel motioned to Buddy, who was across the yard, digging in the snow. "I thought you were going to teach him to behave. Where's that whistle Orlie gave you?"

"It's right here in my jacket." Jacob reached into his pocket, but pulled out an empty hand. "Oh no," he mumbled.

"What?"

"There's a hole in my pocket." Jacob's face turned red as a tomato. "I'm afraid I've lost the whistle."

"You lost it?" Rachel stared at Buddy, who was wagging his tail. "How can you train that mutt not to chase my cat if you don't have the whistle?"

Jacob rubbed his chin. "I don't know when the whistle fell out of my pocket, so I don't know where to look."

Rachel frowned. "I think the dog needs to go back to Orlie. He's out of control."

Jacob's eyes started to water. Rachel didn't know if it was due to the cold or if Jacob was getting teary-eyed because he didn't want to get rid of Buddy.

"I know what I'll do." Jacob moved to Buddy and patted his head. "The next time I go to town, I'll buy Buddy a new whistle!"

Chapter 6

Lots of Snow

Rachel pressed her nose against the living room window. Huge snowflakes drifted past the glass, whirling, swirling, spiraling toward the ground. More snowflakes piled on top of them. In some places the heavy snow had already made snowdrifts.

"I think we might be in for a blizzard," Mom said, stepping beside Rachel.

A few months ago, Rachel remembered seeing a wooly worm, more brown than black, crawling on the fence. Grandpa had said seeing a worm that color meant heavy snow would come soon. Rachel had never heard that about a wooly worm before, but she figured Grandpa must know what he was talking about because he had lived many years.

"Do you really think we'll have a blizzard?" Rachel asked her mother.

Mom nodded. "The way the snow's falling so fast, and the wind's blowing with such powerful gusts, I'd say we're in for a good winter storm." She moved away from the window and stood with her back to the stone fireplace, where a cozy fire lapped at the logs and spilled warmth into the room. "If the weather gets bad enough, school might close until it improves."

Rachel joined Mom in front of the fireplace. If school closed, she wouldn't have any homework to do. Maybe she could sleep in every morning and spend her days playing with Cuddles or painting animal bodies on some of the rocks she found last summer.

"We can't do anything about the weather right now," Mom said, squeezing Rachel's shoulder. "Rudy and Esther are joining us for supper tonight, so I need your help in the kitchen."

Rachel sighed. It seemed like all she did was work, work, work. But she *was* glad to hear that Esther and her husband would come over tonight. Esther had missed their last church service because she was sick, and Rachel looked forward to spending time with her older sister. Esther had always listened to Rachel. She didn't call her "little bensel," the way Jacob often did, either.

"Wash your hands and set the table while I start cooking the noodles," Mom said when she and Rachel entered the kitchen.

Rachel went to the sink. "What else are we having besides noodles?"

"There's a ham in the oven, and we'll have boiled peas, tossed green salad, and hot rolls," Mom replied.

Rachel licked her lips as she lathered her hands with

soap and water. "Just thinking about all that good food makes my stomach hungry."

Mom chuckled. "It seems you're always hungry, Rachel."

"Not when I'm *grank* [sick]."

"That's true," Mom agreed. "Most people aren't in the mood for food when they feel sick."

Rachel remembered when Mom first found out she was going to have a baby. Mom had often felt sick to her stomach. She'd called it "the morning sickness," and said she wasn't in the mood for food.

Mom stirred the boiling noodles on the stove then faced Rachel. "When your grandpa went to take a nap earlier this afternoon, he said I should wake him before Rudy and Esther arrive." She handed the wooden spoon to Rachel. "Would you please watch the noodles while I see if he's awake?"

"How about if I wake Grandpa?" Rachel didn't want to watch the noodles. What if she did something wrong? She didn't look forward to more of Jacob's teasing.

"When I was making the salad earlier, I smeared some tomato juice on my dress," Mom said. "I need to change before our company arrives, and since Grandpa's room is just down the hall from mine, it's easy for me to stop and wake him up."

"Okay, but what should I do if the noodles get done before you get back?" Rachel asked.

"Do you remember how I told you to tell if the noodles are done?"

Rachel nodded. "If I can cut them easily with the spoon, they're tender enough."

"That's right," said Mom. "If they get done before I come back, drain the water into the sink, put the noodles into a bowl, and mix them with a little butter and cheese."

"I think I can do that." Rachel decided the procedure didn't sound too hard. Besides, it shouldn't take Mom long to change her dress and wake Grandpa. She was sure Mom would return before the noodles were done.

"You'll do fine, Rachel." Mom said as she hurried from the room.

Rachel moved to the stove and watched the boiling noodles. Every few seconds she poked the spoon inside and stirred the noodles to keep them from sticking. Mom still wasn't back yet, so when the noodles felt tender, Rachel removed the kettle from the stove. Then she took out the strainer, placed it in the sink, and poured the noodles in.

"Oops!" Most of the noodles missed the strainer and landed in the sink.

"*Sis nau futsch!* [It's all ruined now!]" Rachel muttered as she stared at the noodles. "What should I do?"

Suddenly, an idea popped into Rachel's head. She scooped up the noodles, put them back into the strainer, and turned on the faucet and rinsed them. Next, she took a clean bowl from the cupboard, and poured the noodles into it.

Rachel didn't want anyone to know what had

happened. The sink was clean, she had rinsed the noodles—they shouldn't have any germs on them now.

When Rachel and her family gathered around the kitchen table that evening, Rudy commented on how good everything smelled.

"I agree," Esther put in. "It looks and smells *appeditlich* [delicious]. Mom outdid herself on this meal."

Mom smiled at Rachel. "I can't take all the credit. Rachel cooked the noodles."

"I love hot buttered noodles with plenty of cheese," Rudy said as he forked some into his mouth. He chewed the noodles a couple of times, and a strange expression crossed his face.

"Rudy, what's wrong?" Esther asked. "I thought you liked noodles."

Rudy opened his mouth and pulled out something that didn't look anything like a noodle. It was yellow and square.

"What in all the world?" Mom's glasses slipped to the end of her nose as she studied the small object in Rudy's hand. "Why, that looks like part of the sponge I use for washing dishes!"

Grandpa nodded. "That's what it looks like to me."

Pap turned to Rachel and frowned. "Do you know how part of a sponge got in with the noodles?"

Rachel's face heated. She wished she could crawl under the table and hide. "Well, I—"

"I'll bet she dumped the noodles on the floor and was

trying to wash them with the sponge," Jacob said.

"Please say that's not what happened." Mom's forehead wrinkled as she stared at Rachel. "If you dropped the noodles on the floor, then you should have thrown them out and started over with a new batch."

Rachel shook her head. "I didn't drop them on the floor."

"Then what happened?" Henry wanted to know.

"I was draining the water from the noodles into the strainer." Rachel drew in a quick breath. "But the noodles fell into the sink instead."

"Then what did you do?" Pap questioned.

"I scooped up the noodles, put them back in the strainer, and rinsed them off. Then I took a clean bowl from the cupboard and poured the noodles in." Rachel's ears burned with embarrassment, and her throat felt so tight she could barely swallow. Why was it that every time she tried to do something grownup she made a mess of things?

"I guess you didn't rinse the noodles well enough. Maybe you should have thrown them out and started over," Esther said gently.

"I didn't want to waste them or cause dinner to be late." Rachel shrugged. "I was afraid Mom would be mad if I threw them out."

Grandpa's bushy gray eyebrows lifted high on his forehead. "Maybe you should have waited until your mamm came back to the kitchen to tell you what to do."

Rachel lowered her head and mumbled, "Jah."

Jacob nudged Rachel's arm with his elbow. "And you wonder why I call you a little bensel?"

"Jacob, that's all we need to hear from you on the subject," Pap said. "Rachel feels bad enough about Rudy nearly eating a piece of sponge. You don't have to make her feel any worse."

"If she didn't think she had to be in control of everything. . ."

"Jacob. . ." Pap leaned closer to Jacob and squinted his eyes. "Do you want extra chores to do?"

"No, Pap."

"Then eat your meal and be quiet."

Any other time, Rachel might have found satisfaction in Jacob being scolded for teasing her. Not this time, though. She only wanted to find a place to hide and forget she'd ever been asked to watch the boiling noodles.

"May I be excused?" she asked.

"If you don't finish your supper, you can have no dessert," Mom said.

Rachel shrugged. "I don't care. I'm not hungry."

"Suit yourself; but remember, breakfast is a long time off," Pap said.

Rachel pushed back her chair and stood. Then she turned to Rudy. "I–I'm sorry about the sponge you almost ate." Without waiting for a reply, Rachel rushed out of the room. When she reached the hallway she grabbed her jacket and hurried out the back door.

As Rachel stepped into the snowy yard, her feet went numb from the cold. She should have put on her boots.

"I'll be okay if I hurry," Rachel muttered as she crunched through the snow and headed for the barn. If she found Cuddles there, maybe the two of them could stay warm together by burrowing in a clump of hay.

But she didn't see Cuddles—just Jacob's sleeping dog in the empty horse stall where Jacob was told to keep him until Pap found the time to build a dog house. Rachel was glad Buddy was sleeping. She didn't want to deal with him barking, jumping, or licking her face.

She sat on a bale of hay and closed her jacket tightly. "Sometimes I wish I wasn't me," she mumbled. "Sometimes I wish—"

The barn door swung open, and Esther stepped in. "I thought I might find you here."

Rachel only nodded.

"I came to tell you good-bye," Esther said.

"You're leaving already?"

"Jah. It's snowing much harder now, and Rudy thinks we should head for home before the roads get too bad."

"That's probably a good idea," Rachel agreed.

Esther sat beside Rachel. "I wanted to tell you one more thing."

"What's that?" Rachel asked.

"Don't let Jacob get under your skin. He just likes to tease."

"Jah, I know."

Esther slipped her arm around Rachel's shoulders. "I love you, little sister."

"I love you, too."

When Rachel woke up the following morning, she hurried to the window and lifted the shade. Everything in the yard was white, and the heavy swirling snowflakes kept her from seeing the barn.

Rachel rushed from her room and scrambled down the stairs in her bare feet. "It looks like we got that blizzard you said was coming!" she hollered as she darted into the kitchen and found Mom scrambling some eggs.

"Quiet down, Rachel." Mom put a finger to her lips. "Grandpa's still sleeping."

"Sorry." Rachel peered out the kitchen window. "The snow is so deep I can't even see the path leading from the house to the barn."

"I know," said Mom. "Deacon Byler stopped by a few minutes ago and said they've decided to close the school until the weather improves."

Rachel jumped up and down; then she did a half-spin. "Yippee! That means I have the whole day to play in the snow!"

Mom shook her head. "It's much too cold to play outside."

"But what will I do all day?" Rachel hoped Mom didn't give her more chores. She'd had enough of those.

"Maybe after breakfast you and Jacob can play table games," Mom suggested.

"Let's play checkers," Jacob said, as he stepped into the room.

Rachel frowned. "I don't like playing checkers."

"That's because you always lose."

Rachel squinted at Jacob. "I do not."

Jacob folded his arms. "Okay then. Prove it, right after breakfast!"

"It's nice to stay home from school today," Jacob said as he placed the checkerboard on the folding table in the living room. "This will be *snow* much fun!"

"Ha!" Rachel wrinkled her nose. "Very funny."

Jacob handed her the red checker pieces, and he took the black ones. "You can go first."

"Really?"

He nodded. "Said so, didn't I?"

Rachel made her first move and leaned back in her chair as she waited for Jacob to take his turn. "I hope the storm doesn't last too long. It's fun to be out of school for a day, but I wouldn't want to be cooped up in the house for too long."

"I'm sure the storm won't last forever." Jacob moved his checker piece. "You need to learn to be more patient."

Rachel didn't answer. Her mind was on the game, and how she hoped to win this time. She slid a red checker to the next square. "Your turn, Jacob."

"I know it's my turn. I'm thinking."

"Well, don't think too long. I don't have all day."

"Are you going somewhere?"

"No, I'm not." Rachel shivered and rubbed her hands over her arms. "*Brr*. . .even with a fire in the fireplace, this room seems awfully chilly."

"That's because it's cold outside." Jacob moved his checker piece. "Your turn."

"If it weren't for snow, I wouldn't have landed in the creek when I went sledding a few weeks ago," Rachel grumbled as she moved another checker piece. "I hate the snow!"

"You hate the snow? Since when?"

"I hate it when I have to stay inside and can't play in it."

"Mom says we should never hate anything," Jacob said.

"We're not supposed to hate *anyone*, not *anything*," Rachel corrected.

Jacob stared at Rachel. "Now how did the girl who flunked her history test a few weeks ago get to be so schmaert?"

"I've always been smart. I just don't like history."

"Are you saying you hate history?"

"No, I'm saying I don't *like* history."

"Whatever." Jacob gestured to the checkerboard. "Are you gonna move or not?"

"It's not my turn—it's yours."

A blank expression crossed Jacob's face, and Rachel gritted her teeth. Finally, Jacob picked up a black checker piece and—*click, click, click*—he jumped three of Rachel's red pieces.

"Now who likes to be in control?" she muttered as she took her turn.

"What was that?"

"Oh nothing."

"The only bad part about this blizzard," Jacob said, changing the subject back to the weather, "is that I won't be able to go to town and buy a new whistle for Buddy."

Buddy. Rachel frowned. Did they have to spoil the day by talking about that mutt?

"You still don't like Buddy, do you?" Jacob asked.

She shrugged. "He never listens to me, and he always chases my cat."

"I'll train him—you'll see. As soon as the snow lets up and Pap goes to town, I'll get that whistle. Then once I train Buddy, I'm sure he'll stop chasing Cuddles."

Rachel wasn't convinced that blowing a whistle could make a dog come to someone or stop running. "We'll have to wait and see how it goes," she muttered.

As the game continued, Rachel became more agitated and impatient with Jacob. He took forever to make a move, and since he was obviously winning, she wanted the game to be over. With an exasperated sigh, she reached across the board, picked up one of Jacob's black checker pieces and jumped four of her red pieces. "There!" she announced. "You win the game!"

Chapter 7

Grandpa's Secret

I am so bored. There's nothing fun to do," Rachel complained as she and Jacob sat at the kitchen table drinking the hot chocolate Mom fixed before she went to her room to take a nap. Grandpa was in his room resting, too. Pap and Henry had gone to the buggy shed to repair a broken wheel.

Jacob wrinkled his forehead. "I can't believe school's already been closed for three days on account of the snow."

"The last time I looked out the window, the snow had stopped and the wind wasn't howling so much," Rachel said. "Maybe tomorrow school will be open again."

"I hope so." Jacob poked at the marshmallow floating on top of his cup. "Maybe we could play a game."

Rachel groaned. "Not checkers, please!"

He shook his head. "We could work on a puzzle."

"That takes too much time, and I never can find any of the end pieces."

"Then let's play hide-and-seek."

Rachel blew on her hot chocolate. "That would mean we'd have to run around the house looking for hiding places, which is not a good idea." She glanced at Grandpa's bedroom door down the hall. "We'll be in trouble if we wake Grandpa. We wouldn't want to wake Mom, either."

"That's true," Jacob agreed. "Mom needs her rest because she's expecting a boppli. Grandpa's old, so he needs his rest, too."

"Grandpa's not old," Rachel said with a shake of her head. "And don't you go saying he's going to die soon, either, because—"

Jacob held up his hand. "Who said anything about dying? I was only saying that Grandpa needs more rest because he's. . . Oh, never mind."

Rachel figured Jacob was just looking for an argument, so she changed the subject. "What other games could we play?"

Jacob tapped his fingers on the edge of the table. "Let's see. . . We could play Sorry."

Rachel shook her head. "You always cheat."

"Do not."

"Do so."

"All right," Jacob said, "you choose a game."

"How about Scrabble?" Rachel suggested.

"No way! You always win!"

"That's because I'm a good speller."

"Jah, you're one of the best spellers in our school. Not like me," Jacob mumbled. "I can barely spell my name."

Rachel poked Jacob's arm. "That's not so, and you know it."

He scooted his chair away from the table. "I still think we should play hide-and-seek."

"I told you before, we can't play that in the house." Rachel shook her head. "And we can't play it outside because it's too cold."

"How about the barn?" Jacob asked hopefully. "There are lots of good places to hide in Pap's barn."

"You're right!" Rachel jumped up and grabbed her jacket from the wall peg. "The barn will be a great place to play hide-and-seek!"

"Do you want to hide first or should I?" Jacob asked Rachel when they entered the barn.

"I guess I will." Rachel glanced around. "Where's Buddy? I don't want to hide near him."

"Buddy's a nice dog," Jacob said. "And he really does like you, Rachel."

"No, he doesn't."

"Jah, he does. Why do you think he likes to jump up and lick your face?"

Rachel scrunched up her nose. "It's so *ekelhaft*

[disgusting] when he does that!"

"I've been working with him, and I think he's getting better."

"Humph! He still chases Cuddles."

Jacob heaved a sigh. "I know. I've tried feeding them together, but Buddy eats Cuddles's food, and then she hisses and swipes at his tail."

"That's because she doesn't like him."

"She will someday—hopefully after I buy Buddy a new whistle and train him."

Rachel grunted. "We'll see about that."

"So, are we gonna play hide-and-seek or not?" Jacob asked.

"I suppose so. . . As long as your dog doesn't bark and give away my hiding place."

"I put Buddy in the empty horse stall after I took him for a walk this morning."

"I'll bet it was hard trying to walk him in the snow." Rachel thought about the day Buddy had dragged her facedown in the freezing snow.

"It wasn't so bad." Jacob motioned to the rope hanging from the loft overhead. "I think I'll see if I can hang upside down on that while I count to one hundred and you look for a good place to hide."

Rachel looked up at the rope. Then she looked at Jacob and shook her head. "You're kidding, right?"

"No, I'm not." Jacob scampered up the ladder leading to the hayloft, grabbed the rope, and swung out over the pile of hay near Rachel. "Yippee! This is *snow* much fun!" he shouted. "Maybe I'll forget about playing hide-and-seek and swing on the rope."

Rachel planted her hands on her hips and scowled. "What am I supposed to do while you're swinging?"

"You can play with your cat." Jacob made another pass near Rachel, and as his feet touched the hayloft again, he called, "But that might be hard to do because she's up here sleeping!"

Rachel grunted. "Jacob Yoder, come down here right now! You promised we could play hide-and-seek, and you should never go back on a promise."

"I didn't promise; I just suggested it." He peered at her with a silly grin.

"Fine then—don't play!" Rachel folded her arms and stuck out her lower lip. "See if I care."

"Oh, all right, but I'm going to start counting from here." Still clinging to the rope, Jacob flipped upside down. His face turned crimson from the blood that had rushed to his head.

Rachel rolled her eyes toward the roof of the barn. "Now who's a bensel?"

"You are, little sister!" Jacob closed his eyes. "I'm starting to count now, so you'd better get going. One. . . two. . .three. . ."

Rachel scampered off in search of the best place to hide. *Should I hide in the loft? No, Jacob will hear me climb the ladder. Should I hide in the empty stall? No way! Buddy's in there, and he'll bark and give me away.*

Rachel spotted several bales of hay stacked in one corner. *That looks like a good place to hide!* She tiptoed across the floor and slipped behind them. Now she only had to wait for Jacob to find her.

Jacob finally quit counting, and Rachel tried to be as still as possible. She wondered how long it would take him to discover her hiding place.

Several minutes went by but no sign of Jacob. She didn't hear him walking anywhere, either.

More time passed. Still no Jacob.

Rachel tapped her foot impatiently. *What could be keeping him?*

She twirled her finger around the ties on her *kapp* [cap] and yawned. *Why hasn't he found me yet? What is taking him so long?*

Rachel bit the end of her nail. *If he doesn't find me soon, I won't play this game anymore.*

Several more minutes passed, and Rachel decided she had waited long enough. She slipped out from behind the bales of hay and stood in the middle of the room.

Whoosh! Jacob swept past her, still hanging onto the rope. This time he was right side up.

"Rachel! What are you doing out here?" he hollered. "You're supposed to be hiding."

"I was hiding, but I got tired of waiting." She clucked her tongue, the way Mom often did. "You're slower than sticky melassich, and you were supposed to be looking for me, not swinging on that rope!"

"I'm not slower than molasses. I just wanted to give you plenty of time to hide." Jacob let go of the rope and dropped into the mound of hay below. "*You*, little bensel, are just too impatient!"

Rachel opened her mouth to defend herself, but Pap stepped into the barn and asked Jacob to help him and Henry clean the horses' stalls.

With shoulders slumped and head down, Jacob headed for the stalls.

I guess Jacob's not having such a good time being out of school, either, Rachel thought as she sat on a stool near the woodstove. She sat with her chin cupped in her hand, thinking about how bored she was and how much she missed school.

Rachel swiveled on the stool and looked at the rope hanging from the rafters. *Maybe I should hang upside down like Jacob did.* She shook her head. *I guess that wouldn't be a good idea since I'm wearing a dress.*

Whoosh! A rush of cold air whipped against Rachel's legs as the barn door opened and Grandpa stepped in.

"What are you doing out here?" he asked, joining Rachel in front of the stove.

"Sitting. Thinking." She folded her arms so she wouldn't be tempted to bite another fingernail. It was a bad habit, Mom had told her often. "Trying to not be bored."

"I have an idea." Grandpa's bushy gray eyebrows

jiggled as he rubbed his hands.

"What's that?"

"Why don't we blow some bubbles?"

Rachel made a sweeping gesture of the barn with her hand. "Here?"

He nodded. "When I was a *buwe* [boy] and wanted something fun to do, I got out my bubble wand and made some remarkable bubbles."

"What's so remarkable about blowing bubbles?" Rachel had a bubble wand Pap had made for her birthday last year, but none of her bubbles had been remarkable.

Grandpa patted Rachel's arm. "I'll be right back with my surprise."

Rachel drummed her fingers along the edge of her stool as she waited for Grandpa to return.

A short time later, Grandpa returned, carrying two bubble wands and a bottle of bubble solution. He set the jar on a shelf and opened the lid. He dipped one wand into the liquid and then the other. Slowly, he blew on the first wand until a bubble formed. Then he blew on the other wand, and another bubble formed. Next, he connected the two bubbles and made two more. By the time he was done, he had a chain of bubbles that looked like a worm.

Rachel clapped her hands. "Grandpa, you've made a wooly worm!"

Grandpa laughed from deep in his throat. "You're

right, Rachel—just like the wooly worms you took to school last fall."

Rachel nodded. "I still can't believe the way Orlie tried to win the race by pushing his wooly worm up the string with his tongue. That was so ekelhaft."

"It was a disgusting thing to do," Grandpa said with a nod. "You know, Rachel, it's not good for people to take control of things just to get their way."

Rachel stared at the floor as heat erupted on her cheeks. Was Grandpa talking about her? Did he think she liked to take control?

"Speaking of Orlie," she said, deciding it might be best to change the subject, "his birthday's coming soon. I need to think of something to give him for a present."

Grandpa blew on the bubbles and sent them sailing across the barn. "Maybe you should pray about it."

"I doubt that God would care about something like that."

"Nothing is too small for God to care about," Grandpa said. "You know, there's something I've been praying about, too."

"Have you been praying that God will melt the snow?"

He chuckled. "No, but maybe I should, so you and Jacob can go back to school."

"I was hoping it would snow really hard so school would be closed, but now I'm ready to go back," Rachel admitted.

"I understand." Grandpa handed Rachel one of the bubble wands. "Can you keep a secret?"

She nodded. She felt grown up to know Grandpa would trust her with his secret.

"The thing that I've been praying about is. . ." Grandpa leaned close to Rachel's ear and whispered, "I'm thinking about opening a greenhouse in the spring."

Rachel's eyes widened. "Really?"

"Jah. I've enjoyed working with flowers ever since I was a boy. Now that I'm older and retired from farming, I want to do something useful with the time I have left on this earth."

"I hope you have lots of time left," Rachel said as a lump formed in her throat. She couldn't imagine not having Grandpa around.

He leaned over and hugged Rachel. "Don't worry. If I take care of myself, I think I'll be with you a long time."

"I like flowers, too, Grandpa. I wish I could own a greenhouse some day." Rachel sighed. "But I guess that will never happen."

"Maybe when you're older and out of school," Grandpa said.

Rachel shook her head. "I doubt I'll ever get to do any of the things I really want to do."

"Besides owning a greenhouse, what else would you like to do?" he asked.

"I'd like to go for a ride in a car that has no top. When I told Jacob that, he said the idea was foolishness."

"You really want to ride in a convertible?"

She nodded.

"Why?"

"I think it would be fun to be in a car with the top down, going really fast." Rachel scrunched her nose. "But I don't know if it'll ever happen, and I'm getting tired of waiting."

"The Bible says in Proverbs 19:11: 'A man's wisdom gives him patience.'" Grandpa patted Rachel's head. "You need more patience, but you also need good judgment."

Rachel tipped her head. "What do you mean?"

"I had an experience once that taught me a lesson I'll never forget," he replied.

"What experience was that?"

Grandpa leaned his head back and closed his eyes. Rachel wondered if he had fallen asleep.

"It was a long time ago. . ." Grandpa said. "I was a teenage boy, like Henry."

Rachel realized now why Grandpa had closed his eyes. He was remembering.

"I wanted to ride a motorcycle. Wanted it more than anything." Grandpa paused, and his lips twitched. "Our English neighbor, Robert, got a motorcycle for his birthday one year, and Robert promised me a ride." He paused again.

Rachel fidgeted with the strings on her kapp. She was anxious for Grandpa to finish his story. "Did you get to take that ride, Grandpa?"

He opened his eyes and blinked. "I took it all right. Robert gave me the ride of my life."

"Did you go really fast?"

Grandpa nodded. "It was the fastest ride I've ever had."

Rachel's eyes widened, and her heart pounded. "Was it fun?"

"It was, until we skidded on some gravel and the motorcycle tipped over." Grandpa's forehead wrinkled. "Robert broke his leg, but I ended up with some nasty cuts and scrapes." He pulled up his pant leg and pointed to a finger-length scar.

Rachel's mouth fell open. "Grandpa, I never knew you did anything like that."

Grandpa nodded soberly. "You have to be careful about the choices you make, Rachel. Don't be in a hurry to experience all the things the world has to offer. Some things aren't as fun as you think they will be." He reached for Rachel's hand and gently squeezed her fingers.

Rachel nestled against Grandpa's shoulder. "I'm glad you came to live with us."

He smiled. "Me, too."

Chapter 8

Always in a Hurry

What are you making?" Jacob asked on Thursday morning when he entered the kitchen, where Rachel sat at the table.

Rachel turned in her chair. "I'm getting ready to paint a ladybug rock for Orlie, and I need to hurry so I can get it done on time."

"*Dummel dich net!* [Take your time, don't hurry!]" Jacob said, shaking his head.

Rachel frowned. "Why do you always tell me what to do?"

"Because you're a little bensel and need someone to tell you what to do."

"I don't need *you* telling me what to do." Rachel flapped her hand at him. "Go away. . .shoo. . .don't bother me."

"No problem. The roads are better today, so Pap hitched one of our buggy horses to the sleigh. I'm going to town with him and Grandpa." Jacob leaned close to

Rachel's ear. "You won't have to put up with me for the rest of the morning, little bensel."

"If you're heading to town, don't forget to buy a whistle so you can train Buddy."

"I won't; that's why I decided to go along." Jacob peered over Rachel's shoulder. "Why are you making a painted rock for Orlie? I thought you didn't like him."

Rachel's cheeks burned. Would Jacob tease her about Orlie now? "I don't like some of the things Orlie does," she said, "but I don't dislike him. Right before Christmas I promised to make something for his birthday, so I'm trying to keep that promise."

Jacob's forehead wrinkled. "You still don't like the fact that Orlie gave me his dog, do you?"

"I don't like Buddy, but I'm not mad at Orlie." Rachel shrugged. "Besides, he had to give the mutt to someone."

Jacob nodded. "Well, I'd better go. I don't want to keep Pap and Grandpa waiting in the cold." *Bam!* Jacob slammed the back door.

Rachel picked up the small paintbrush lying on the table. If she hurried, she might have time to play in the snow.

She dipped her paintbrush in the bottle of black paint and painted the entire rock for the ladybug's body. Then she dipped the brush into the white paint to make the ladybug's eyes and antenna.

"Ach!" Rachel cried when she realized that the white paint had turned gray. "I should have cleaned the black paint off the brush before dipping it into the white paint."

Rachel rushed to the sink and washed out the brush; then hurried back to the table. She dipped the brush into the white paint again and drew a circle for each eye and thin lines for the ladybug's antenna. Now it only needed some red circles on its body for wings, two black dots in the white circles for the eyes, and a red line for the mouth. Then the ladybug rock would be finished.

This time Rachel remembered to wash the brush before she dipped it into the red paint. But she didn't remember to wait until the black paint had dried before adding the red dots to the body.

"Ugh!" she moaned. The red paint had run into the black paint! Now she had to start over again.

Rachel was glad Jacob wasn't there to see her mistake. He probably would have teased her about it and called her a bensel.

Rachel took the rock to the sink and turned on the faucet. Black, red, and white paint dribbled off the rock and ran down the drain. "What a waste," she muttered.

"Rachel, please go outside and give the chickens food and water," Mom said as she stepped into the kitchen.

"Now?"

Mom nodded.

"Can't it wait until I finish painting Orlie's ladybug rock?"

Mom shook her head. "The chickens need to be cared for."

"Okay." Rachel placed the rock on the edge of the sink and dried her hands on a towel. At this rate, she would never get to play in the snow.

She slipped into her jacket, and was almost to the back door, when Mom called, "While you're outside, you'd better go to the barn and give Jacob's dog some food and water."

Rachel frowned. "Didn't Jacob do that before he left for town?"

Mom shook her head. "Your daed was in a hurry so Jacob asked Henry to give food and water to Buddy."

"Then why are you asking me to do it?"

"Because I asked Henry to chop wood for the stove, and he'll be busy with that for quite awhile," Mom said. "Since you're going outside, I figured you could tend to Buddy."

Rachel wasn't happy about doing anything for Buddy, but she knew better than to argue. "Okay," she mumbled.

"And don't forget to take a bucket of hot water with you, because the water dishes in the chicken coop are probably frozen."

Rachel found a bucket in the utility room, filled it with hot water from the sink, and headed out the door. She walked carefully through the snow so she wouldn't spill any water. Besides the fact that it was hot, Rachel knew if she got any on her clothes, it could freeze right on the spot. The last thing she needed was to burn herself, or end up with a cold, frozen dress!

When Rachel entered the chicken coop, she discovered that the water in all the dishes was frozen, just as Mom had said. Carefully, she poured hot water over the ice. When it melted enough for the chickens to drink, she opened the bag of chicken feed and put some in each food dish.

When that was done, Rachel picked up the empty bucket and turned to go. She'd only taken a few steps, when—*whack!*—she was hit in the leg by the wing of a squawking chicken. Another hen squawked and soon the whole chicken coop became a whirl of noisy, flapping chickens.

Gripping the empty bucket, Rachel dashed for the door. She didn't look forward to returning to the chicken coop, but knew she would be expected to feed and water the chickens again tomorrow.

Rachel stepped outside and walked slowly across the yard. When she entered the barn she heard a whistling, snorting sound coming from the stall where Buddy slept. She set the bucket on the floor, hurried to the other side of the barn, and slowly opened the stall door. The last thing she needed was for Buddy to see her and get all excited.

As soon as Rachel saw Buddy, curled up in a mound of straw, she recognized the whistling, snorting sound. Buddy was snoring!

She held her breath and tiptoed across the floor, careful not to wake the sleeping dog. Then she picked up

Buddy's empty water dish and left the stall.

When Rachel reached the other side of the barn, she set the dish on the floor and grabbed the hose Pap used to clean things in the barn. The hose was connected to a water pipe, and during the cold winter months, Pap kept a lantern lit above the pipe so it wouldn't freeze.

Rachel leaned over, and was about to turn on the faucet, when—*fump!*—two big paws landed on her back and nearly pushed her over.

Rachel whirled around and shook her finger at Buddy. "Stay down! You almost knocked me down, you big, hairy mutt!" She would be glad when Jacob got home with a new whistle.

Buddy tipped his head to one side and whined.

"You should be ashamed of yourself, Buddy," she muttered.

The dog nudged Rachel with his cold, wet nose, the way he did when he wanted to play. She wished she'd remembered to close the stall door, but she hadn't expected Buddy to wake up while she was filling his water dish.

"I don't have time to play now." Rachel grunted. "I only came here to give you some food and water."

Buddy's tongue shot out, and he licked Rachel's hand.

"Stop that!" She wiped her hand on her jacket and turned on the hose. When Buddy's dish was full of water, she carried it carefully back to his stall. Buddy followed and lapped at the water as soon as she set the dish on the floor.

Rachel put food in Buddy's dish; then she closed the stall door and headed out of the barn.

She tromped through the snow toward the house but halted when several snowflakes brushed her cheeks. "I hope we don't have another snowstorm," Rachel said with a groan. She needed to get Orlie's rock painted, and then she hoped to build a snowman.

The snow stopped as quickly as it had started, and when Rachel looked up, she realized the flakes of snow she'd felt had dropped from the tree overhead, not from the sky.

Rachel stared longingly at the ground, glistening with tiny ice crystals. It would be so much fun to make a pretty snow angel. If she was going to get Orlie's rock done today, she shouldn't take the time to play in the snow, but—well, maybe she could make just one snow angel.

Rachel dropped to the ground, spread her arms back and forth, and stared at the hazy sky. Of all the seasons, she liked summer the best, but there were some fun things to do in the winter.

Yip! Yip! Yip! Rachel thoughts were interrupted as Buddy carried on in the barn.

She moaned and clambered to her feet. "Now what is that dog's problem? He's been fed and watered; I thought he might go back to sleep."

Rachel glanced at the barn and gasped. Water ran out from under the barn door and formed a puddle in the yard!

"Oh no," she moaned. "I must have left the hose running!"

Stepping around the water, which seemed to freeze right before Rachel's eyes, she rushed into the barn. Sure enough, the hose was still running, and water ran everywhere.

"The hurrier I go, the behinder I get," Rachel mumbled. That was one of Grandma Yoder's favorite sayings. "Why, oh why, did I leave that hose running?"

Rachel sloshed her way over to the sink and turned off the water. Then, being careful to stay away from the frozen puddle outside, she started for the house.

Woof! Woof! Buddy bounded up to her, barking and wagging his tail.

"How did you get out?" Rachel scolded. She'd thought she had closed both the stall door and the barn door. She shook her head slowly and frowned. "Everything's so *verhuddelt* [mixed up] today."

As Rachel stepped forward, her foot slipped on the ice, and she grabbed Buddy's collar to keep from falling.

Buddy must have thought she wanted to play because he took off like a shot. Slipping and sliding over the frozen water and into the snowy yard, he pulled Rachel along.

"Stop, Buddy!" she hollered. But Buddy kept going.

Around and around in circles he went, like an ice skater. Rachel's stomach flew up and her head spun like a top. This was not the kind of fun she'd planned to have today!

Buddy screeched to a stop, and Rachel plopped into a mound of snow.

Slurp! Slurp! The unruly dog licked her face with his big red tongue.

Rachel scrambled to her feet. "Bad dog! Jacob needs to teach you some manners!"

Buddy whimpered and lowered his head.

Rachel clomped up the stairs and rushed into the kitchen.

"Slow down, Rachel," Mom said. "What's your hurry?"

Before Rachel could reply, Buddy bolted into the room, circled Rachel, and crashed into the table. Rachel's jars of paint toppled over, and a pool of red, black, and white paint dripped onto the floor.

"Oh no!" Rachel wailed. "Now I can't paint a ladybug rock for Orlie's birthday!"

Mom grabbed Buddy's collar and ushered him out the door; then she turned to Rachel. "Why did you let Jacob's dog in the house?"

"I—I didn't. He followed me up to the house, after I—" Tears sprang to Rachel's eyes. "Oh, Mom, everything I've tried to do this morning has gone wrong!"

"Besides this mess, what else has gone wrong?" Mom

asked, motioning to the paint.

Rachel grabbed a mop to clean the paint, while she told Mom about the trouble in the chicken coop, the barn, and then outside with the ice and Buddy dragging her across the slippery yard.

"It sounds to me like you could have avoided at least some of that trouble if you hadn't been in such a hurry." Mom clucked her tongue. "It doesn't pay to be impatient or to try to do things too quickly."

"I wanted to hurry so I could paint Orlie's rock, and then I hoped I could play in the snow." Rachel drew in a quick breath. "Now I have no paint left, so I can't give Orlie a rock for his birthday."

"Why don't you give Orlie one of your own painted rocks?" Mom suggested.

Rachel sniffed. "I—I do have that ladybug rock in my room. I guess I could give it to Orlie and make a new one for myself when I get more paint."

Mom smiled and patted Rachel's head. "That would be a nice thing to do."

Just then, the back door opened, and Jacob stepped into the house. "Whew! It was sure cold riding in that sleigh!" he said, rubbing his hands together.

"Where's your daed and Grandpa?" Mom questioned.

"In the barn, putting the horse away."

"Would you like some hot chocolate?" Mom asked.

Jacob nodded. "That sounds good."

Mom scurried to the stove. "I'd better put some

coffee on for the menfolk. It'll warm them when they come inside."

Rachel stepped up to Jacob. "Did you get the whistle for Buddy?"

He reached into his jacket pocket and withdrew a shiny plastic whistle. "Sure did. And this time I didn't lose it, because Mom patched the hole in my pocket."

"When are you going to try it out on Buddy?" Rachel asked.

"I'll probably wait until Saturday."

"Why not now?" she asked.

He slipped out of his jacket and rubbed his hands over his arms. "I'm too cold to work with Buddy right now, and later today I'm supposed to go to Grandma and Grandpa Yoder's to help Grandpa clean his barn."

"What about tomorrow?" she asked.

Jacob shook his head. "We saw Deacon Byler in town, and he said the schoolhouse will be open again tomorrow."

Rachel smiled. "Oh, that's good. I'm more than ready to go back to school."

"Jah, me, too."

"So can't you work with Buddy tomorrow after school?"

"I don't think so. Pap said something about my helping Henry groom the horses."

Rachel's smile turned to a frown. At this rate, Buddy would never be trained!

As Rachel headed to school the next day, she felt good about what she had in her coat pocket.

"Why are you wearing such a silly grin?" Jacob asked. "Are you glad we're going to school?"

She nodded and quickened her steps, careful not to step on any icy patches. When she entered the schoolyard, she spotted Orlie by the swings, building a snowman.

She pulled the ladybug rock out of her pocket and hoped no one would see her give the rock to Orlie. She was almost there when her foot slipped on a patch of ice. The rock flew out of Rachel's hand, and she landed face-down in a pile of snow.

"What happened?" Orlie asked, pulling Rachel to her feet.

"I was coming to give you—" She clamped her hand over her mouth. "Oh no—I lost it!"

Orlie's eyebrows drew together. "What did you lose?"

"Your birthday present. I dropped it in the *schnee* [snow]."

"You brought me a birthday present?"

She nodded. "It's one of my painted ladybug rocks."

"Let's look for it." Orlie dropped to his knees and pawed through the snow, like a dog trying to cover a bone. Rachel did the same. Snow flew to the left. Snow flew to the right. No ladybug rock was in sight.

"I think it's lost," Rachel mumbled.

Orlie grinned at Rachel as he helped her to her feet.

"It's okay. When the snow melts, I'm sure we'll find my birthday present."

Rachel smiled. She was glad Orlie was so understanding.

"How's Buddy getting along?" Orlie asked as they walked toward the schoolhouse.

"Well, he's—"

"I've been meaning to get over to your place to see him," Orlie interrupted, "but something's always prevented me from coming."

"Like what?" Rachel wanted to know.

"First my daed came down with the flu, so I had twice as many chores. Then it was the bad weather." Orlie's forehead wrinkled. "Maybe it's best if I don't see Buddy. It might make me miss him more than I already do."

"If you miss the dog so much, maybe you should take him back," Rachel said as she and Orlie stepped onto the schoolhouse porch.

"I can't. My mamm's allergic to Buddy, remember?"

Rachel nodded.

"So, how is Buddy doing? Is he happy living at your place?"

"He seems happy enough, but he chases my cat and won't come when he's called."

Orlie's eyebrows drew together. "Isn't Jacob using the whistle I gave him?"

Rachel explained how Jacob had lost the whistle but had bought a new one for Buddy yesterday. "Jacob thinks he can train Buddy better now that he has a new whistle," she added.

"I think he's right," Orlie said, nodding. "Using a whistle with Buddy always worked for me."

Rachel opened her lunch pail, pulled out a plump winter pear, and handed it to him. "This isn't the present I'd planned to give you today, but happy birthday, Orlie!"

Chapter 9

A *Dappich* Day

Are you sure you don't want to go shopping with me and your daed?" Mom asked Rachel as she wrapped a large woolen shawl around her shoulders.

"Why are you going shopping? I thought Pap, Grandpa, and Jacob went shopping on Thursday."

Mom shook her head. "Not exactly. They went to town to pick up a new harness your daed ordered. Today we'll shop for groceries."

"I see."

"So do you want to go along?"

Rachel shook her head. "Since today's Saturday and there's still plenty of snow, I thought it would be fun to build a snowman."

"You could do that after we get home from town."

"I'd rather play in the snow than shop."

"Very well." Mom smiled. "Grandpa and Jacob are staying home, so if you need anything while we're gone, you can ask them."

"Where will Henry be?" Rachel questioned. "Is he going shopping with you?"

"Henry left a while ago," Mom said. "He went to see his *aldi* [girlfriend], Nancy."

Rachel wrinkled her nose. "I hope Henry doesn't get married and leave us, the way Esther did last fall."

Mom shook her head. "Henry's only seventeen—too young for marriage. Besides, it's not like we never see Esther. She and Rudy only live a few miles away."

"Jah, I know."

"I'd better get outside. I'm sure your daed has the horse and buggy ready to go by now." Mom opened the back door. "Be good while we're gone, Rachel."

"I will." Rachel closed the door behind her mother and hurried to the utility room to put on her boots. She could hardly wait to get outside!

"Would you like to help me build a snowman?" Rachel called to Jacob when she stepped outside and saw him walking toward the barn.

"Maybe later. I'm going to train Buddy right now. I want to try the whistle I bought him the other day."

"Okay, but please don't let him out of the barn," Rachel hollered. "I don't want that mutt running all over the place. He might wreck my snowman."

"What snowman? I don't see a snowman." Jacob cupped his hands around his eyes, like he was looking through binoculars. "But I do see a *schneeballe* [snowball] coming."

He scooped up a handful of snow and flung it at Rachel.

Whizz!—the white sphere hit Rachel's arm with a *splat!* Jacob leaned his head back and laughed.

"Very funny!" Rachel grabbed some snow. She packed it into a snowball, and was ready to hurl it at Jacob, when he disappeared into the barn.

"That figures," Rachel mumbled as she squatted, ready to make the lower half of her snowman.

By the time Rachel had made a good-sized snowball and rolled it big enough for the bottom of the snowman's body, she was out of breath. "Whew! This is hard work," she panted. "I wish someone would help me."

Rachel thought about asking Grandpa, but knew he was taking a nap. Besides, the cold air would probably bother his arthritis.

She stood there until her toes throbbed. "I'd better keep moving," she told herself.

Rachel grabbed a wad of snow in her hands. Even through her woolen gloves, she could feel the biting cold as she packed it into a ball. *Push. Roll. Push. Roll.* Rachel pushed and rolled the snowball around the yard until it was the size she needed.

"Umph!" Rachel grunted as she tried to lift the snowball and set it on the lower half of the body. She'd made it too big. Now she couldn't even pick it up.

"Now what?" Rachel glanced at the barn. No sign of Jacob. *He must still be trying to train that troublesome dog. Guess I'll have to go ask him to help me.*

Rachel trudged through the snow, opened the barn door, and called, "Jacob, where are you?"

"I'm in here, working with Buddy," he said from the empty stall.

When Rachel stepped into the stall, she found Jacob kneeling on the floor beside Buddy. "How's it going?"

He shook his head. "Not so good. Look what happens when I blow on the whistle." Jacob led Buddy to one side of the barn, and then he went to the other side and blew the whistle. "Come, Buddy, come!"

Buddy didn't budge. He tipped his head back and howled. *Aw-oo-oo!*

"I didn't think a silly old whistle would make Buddy listen," Rachel said.

"He needs more time." Jacob held up the whistle. "This probably has a different sound than the whistle Orlie gave me. I'm sure sooner or later Buddy will get used to it and do what he's supposed to do."

"It will probably be later," Rachel muttered.

"Why did you come to the barn?" Jacob asked. "Did you give up on your snowman?"

"No, but I need your help putting the middle section of the snowman in place."

"Can't you do it?"

She shook her head. "I made it too big, and it's too heavy for me to pick up."

"Don't go anywhere, Buddy; I'll be right back." Jacob patted Buddy's head and stood. "Let's go, Rachel."

Soon Rachel and Jacob had the body of the snowman set in place. "Now I only need to make the head," she said.

"The head won't need to be as big, so you won't need help for that," Jacob said. "I have to finish training Buddy."

Rachel smiled. "Danki for your help."

"*Gern gschehne.* [You are welcome.]" He trudged through the snowy path toward the barn.

Rachel's excitement mounted as she rolled the ball that would become the snowman's head.

Finally, Rachel had the snowman's head just the right size. She grunted as she lifted it and stood on her tiptoes to set it in place. She couldn't reach. She'd made the snowman's body too tall!

Rachel plodded back to the barn. "Jacob, I need your help again!"

"What now, Rachel?"

"My snowman's body is too tall. I can't reach high enough to set the head in place. Can you help me?"

Jacob groaned. "Can't you see that I'm busy? If you don't stop bothering me, I'll never finish training Buddy."

"Please, Jacob," Rachel pleaded. "I really do need your help."

"Okay. I'll be there as soon as I'm done."

"Danki."

Rachel left the barn and returned to her unfinished

snowman. Her nose and toes grew colder as she waited. . . waited. . .waited. The longer she waited, the more impatient she became. With an exasperated sigh, she finally headed for the house. She returned a few minutes later carrying a small wooden stool. Lifting the snowman's head into her arms, she climbed onto the stool. Then she raised her arms, and—*oof!*—the head slipped out of her hands, landed in the snow, and rolled away.

Rachel hopped off the stool and tromped after the rolling snowball. But it was too late—it had rolled to the edge of the hill behind the house—and down it went!

"My snowman's head!" Rachel shrieked.

Rachel slipped and slid down the snowy hill. When she reached the bottom, she was relieved that the snowman's head hadn't broken. But it had rolled through so much snow it was twice as big as before!

Rachel knew she would never be able to carry the snowman's head back up the hill. Maybe she could roll it.

She groaned. "But if I roll it up the hill, it will make the head grow larger."

"Hey, little bensel! What are you doing down there?"

Rachel looked up. Jacob stood at the top of the hill, staring at her.

"When I tried to put the snowman's head on its body, it slipped off and rolled down the hill," she hollered at him. "Now the head's so big I can't get it back up the hill."

Jacob slid down the hill until he stood beside Rachel. "I said I would help you when I finished working with

Buddy. Why didn't you wait?"

"I got tired of waiting," she replied. "You took too long."

Jacob nudged Rachel with his elbow. "You're just an *ungeduldich* [impatient] little bensel."

"I'm not impatient."

"Jah, you're impatient, and you try to control everything."

"I do not!"

Jacob nodded. "Want me to give you some examples?"

Rachel shook her head. Then she crouched down and started rolling the snowman's head in the snow.

"What are you doing?" Jacob questioned.

"I've decided to turn the snowman's head into a snowman's body here. When I'm done making this snowman, I'll make another head for the snowman in our yard."

"Do you want some help?"

"Jah, sure, but what about Buddy?"

Jacob chuckled. "I don't think he wants to help us build a snowman."

Rachel groaned and rolled her eyes. "I meant, don't you need to keep working with him?"

"Nope. I've given up for the day." Jacob scooped up some snow and started rolling it into a ball. He glanced over his shoulder. "Well, don't just stand there, Rachel. Get another snowball going!"

Rachel was on the verge of telling Jacob that he

wasn't her boss, but she decided to keep quiet. If she said anything, they'd end up arguing, and then Jacob would walk away and leave her to build the snowmen by herself.

Rachel worked silently with Jacob as they made a plump snowman at the bottom of the hill. By the time they were finished, her nose and toes were so cold she could barely feel them.

"It looks pretty good, don't you think?" Jacob folded his arms and stared at the snowman. "All it needs now is a mouth, nose, and eyes."

"And d–don't forget a h–hat." Rachel shivered. She was so cold she was sure her lips were blue.

"You look cold. Should we finish the other snowman tomorrow?" Jacob asked.

"No, I'll be f–fine." Rachel plodded up the hill behind Jacob, huffing and puffing.

"Why don't you go in the house and get carrots for our snowmen's noses?" Jacob suggested. "While you're doing that, I'll make the second snowman's head."

Rachel nodded and hurried to the house. If she stood by the woodstove in the kitchen a few minutes, she might warm up enough to help Jacob finish their snowmen.

She went to the refrigerator and took out two long, skinny carrots. Next, she removed four black buttons from Mom's sewing basket and placed them on the table. Then she removed her gloves and scurried to the woodstove. "Ah, that feels better," she said, holding her hands out to the warmth. She was tempted to take off her boots and thaw out her toes but figured that would take too much time.

Once the numbness in Rachel's fingers went away, she slipped on her gloves and headed for the door. On her way out, she grabbed two straw hats. One was Henry's and one was Pap's. Since it was winter, and the men wouldn't wear their straw hats until spring, Rachel thought it would be okay to use them for the snowmen.

"What took you so long?" Jacob asked when Rachel returned.

"I had to gather things we needed, and I stood by the stove a few minutes."

"Figured as much." He motioned to the snowman. "I put the head on while you were gone, so now we only need to give the icy fellow a face."

Rachel handed Jacob one of the carrots, two buttons, and Pap's straw hat. "Why don't you do the snowman at the bottom of the hill, and I'll do the one here in the yard?"

Jacob squinted at her. "Who put you in charge?"

"No one, but it was my idea to build the snowmen, so—"

"Never mind," he interrupted. "Let's just get this job done before we both freeze." He took the carrot, buttons, and hat from Rachel, and then disappeared over the hill.

Rachel faced the snowman. With the head in place it was taller than she was, but if she used the stool she'd brought out earlier she should be able to reach high enough.

Soon Rachel had the buttons in place for the snowman's eyes, and the carrot for its nose. Then she plunked the straw hat on its head. She climbed down from the stool and stepped back to admire her work. It looked good, but something was missing. The snowman needed a mouth!

Rachel glanced around the yard, wondering what she could use. Maybe a small branch from a tree would work. She reached up to grab a smaller one, but her fingers were too cold to break it.

"What's the matter? Do you have a problem?"

Rachel whirled around at the sound of Jacob's voice. "Don't scare me like that! I thought you were still at the bottom of the hill."

He shook his head. "Nope. That snowman's done. I'm ready to go inside and warm up. How about you?"

"I'll be ready as soon as I give my snowman a mouth." She tugged on the tree branch and frowned. "If I can ever break it, that is."

"Step aside and I'll see what I can do."

Rachel did as Jacob said, and with one quick snap, he broke off a small piece of the branch. "Here you go," he said, handing it to Rachel.

Rachel smiled as she put the snowman's mouth in place. "Danki for your help, Jacob."

"Sure, no problem," he said with nod. "Are you ready to go inside now?"

"I'm more than ready."

When Rachel and Jacob stepped into the house, they hung their coats, gloves, and hats on a wall peg then slipped out of their boots. Rachel was glad her long stockings had stayed dry, but her feet felt so cold she could barely walk.

She plodded to the warm kitchen and sat at the table. "That feels so good," she said as she rested her feet on the chair closest to the woodstove. "Should we have some hot chocolate and cookies?"

Jacob nodded, rubbing his hands briskly together. "Jah, sure. Hot chocolate sounds wunderbaar!"

"Good. Why don't you fix the hot chocolate? I'll get out the cookies as soon as my toes thaw out."

"All right, little bensel," Jacob said, scrunching up his nose, "but I'm only doing it because I'm such a nice *bruder* [brother]."

Rachel was tempted to remind Jacob that he wasn't always nice, but he had helped her build the two snowmen, so she decided to keep quiet.

Soon the two sat across from each other enjoying steaming mugs of hot chocolate and some of Mom's fresh ginger cookies. Rachel listened to the steady *tick-tick-tick* of the kitchen clock. "I wonder what I can do until Mom and Pap get home from town."

"Maybe you should take a nap like Grandpa's doing," Jacob suggested.

She shook her head. "That wouldn't be any fun."

"Maybe you'd like to sit in front of the window and

look out at our big, fat snowman."

"That might be fun, but it would soon become boring."

Jacob snapped his fingers. "I know. . .you could go out to the barn and play with your cat." Before Rachel could response, he added, "Oh, you'd better not. Buddy's in the barn, and if he sees you, he'll jump up and lick your face."

Rachel wrinkled her nose. "I hate it when Buddy does that."

"I've told you, he only does it because he likes you."

"Jah, well, I don't care much for him, and I'm not going to the barn right now," Rachel said with a shake of her head. "I'm staying in here where it's warm."

Jacob pushed away from the table and stood. "I think I'll go back to the barn and work with Buddy some more."

After Jacob left the house, Rachel sat there, staring at her empty cup. Suddenly, an idea popped into her head. "I'll paint a ladybug rock to replace the one I gave Orlie last week!" A few days earlier, Esther had given Rachel some paint, so all Rachel needed was a flat, round rock.

She hurried to her room and searched through the box of rocks in her closet. Sure enough, one was shaped exactly right for a ladybug.

Rachel picked up the paint, a brush, and the rock; then she returned to the kitchen. She covered the table with some old newspapers she'd found in the utility room and removed the lids from the paint jars. She dipped her brush into the jar of black paint and painted the entire rock. While the paint dried, Rachel washed the brush and ate a few more ginger cookies. Now it was time to paint the ladybug's eyes and antenna.

Rachel picked up the jar of white paint, dipped the brush in, and painted a small circle for the first eye. She was about to dip the brush in again, to do the second eye, when—*blurp!*—she hiccupped. A blob of white paint shot up and landed on the front of her dress.

"Oh no!" Rachel jumped up and raced to the sink. She grabbed the wet sponge and blotted the white splotch on her dress, but that only smeared the paint.

"I'd better wash this dress before Mom gets home." Rachel scurried up the stairs to her room, changed into a clean dress, and rushed back to the kitchen. Then she ran warm water into the sink, added some detergent, and dropped the dress in.

Swish! Swish! Swish!—she dipped the dress up and down and swirled it around in the soapy water.

When she was sure the paint was out, she drained the soapy water and ran cold water into the sink. *Swish! Swish! Swish!*—she dipped the dress up and down; then wrung it out. She carried it across the room and hung it over the back of a chair to dry by the stove.

Rachel glanced at the clock. Mom had said she and Pap should be home in time for lunch and it was eleven thirty. If the dress wasn't dry when they got home, Mom would know Rachel had slopped paint on her dress.

"I've got to think of something." Rachel scratched the side of her head. "I need to figure out how to dry my dress quickly."

Another idea popped into Rachel's head. *I know! I'll iron the water out of my dress!*

Rachel hurried to the utility closet and removed the ironing board. She knew it would be too dangerous for her to use the small propane torch to light the wick on the bottom of the iron Mom normally used, so she decided to heat Mom's old flat iron on the stove.

Rachel turned on the gas, and set the iron on the front burner. While the iron heated, she ate another cookie and drank a glass of milk. Then she peeked out the kitchen window. No sign of Pap's buggy. That was good. She glanced down the hall and saw that Grandpa's bedroom door was still closed. He must still be asleep.

Rachel removed the dress from the chair and placed it over the ironing board. When she lifted the iron from the stove and placed it on the dress, it sizzled.

"It's working!" she exclaimed. Rachel held the iron there until the spot was dry. She smiled. "At this rate the dress will be dry in no time at all."

Thump! Thump! Rachel tipped her head and listened. It sounded like someone was tromping down the stairs. But that was impossible. Mom, Pap, and Henry weren't home; Grandpa was asleep in his room; and Jacob was in the barn.

Thump! Thump! Thump! There it was again.

Rachel let go of the iron, raced into the hallway, and screeched to a halt. *Thump-thumpety-thump*—Rachel's cat was dragging a shoe down the stairs.

"Cuddles! Who let you in the house?" Rachel shook her finger at the cat. "And what are you doing with my shoe?"

Meow! Cuddles dropped the shoe and pawed at Rachel's leg.

"Don't 'meow' me," Rachel scolded. "You know better than to play with my shoes. I'll bet you snuck into the house when Jacob went to the barn, didn't you?"

Rachel picked up the cat. "I don't have time to play with you now, so out you go." She opened the back door and set Cuddles on the porch. "Find a warm place in the barn and take a nap." *Bam!* She quickly shut the door.

When Rachel returned to the kitchen, she gasped. A curl of smelly, gray smoke rose from her dress. "Ach!" she screamed. "My dress is burning!"

Rachel lifted the iron and stared in horror at an ugly brown scorch mark. She realized that when she'd gone to see what the *thump-thump-thump* on the stairs was, she'd left the iron on top of her dress.

A horse whinnied outside, and Rachel jumped. Mom and Pap must be home!

Rachel knew it would be impossible to cover the smoke or hide the scorch mark on her dress, so she stood in front of the ironing board and waited.

Mom entered the house. "What's that horrible smell?" she asked, sniffing the air.

Rachel pointed to her ruined dress and burst into tears. "I—I dribbled some paint on the front of my dress." *Sniff.* "Then I washed it in the sink." *Sniff. Sniff.* "I knew it would take too long to dry, so I tried to iron it." *Sniff.* "I heard a noise on the steps." *Sniff. Sniff.* "And when I came back to the kitchen, I'd left the iron on my dress. Now it's ruined!"

Mom slowly shook her head. "Oh, Rachel, don't you know how dangerous it was for you to leave the iron on your dress when you left the room?"

"I know, and I'm so sorry. I was afraid you'd be mad at me for spilling the paint, so I wanted to dry the dress before you got home." Rachel stared at the floor as tears blurred her vision. "Now you're mad at me for scorching the dress." She gulped a sob. "I'm having such a dappich day! I can't do anything right."

"You did the right thing by washing the paint out of the dress so quickly," Mom said, her voice softening. "You just should have been more patient in letting it dry on its own."

Rachel nodded. "I'll save my money to buy material for a new dress."

"That won't be necessary. You can sew a patch over the scorch mark and wear the dress for doing your chores."

Rachel frowned. Even though Mom had given her a sewing kit for her birthday last year, she still couldn't sew very well.

Mom hugged Rachel. "You need to remember we

can't always fix things or make them come out the way we would like. But you can always count on the knowledge that God loves you, and so do I."

Rachel smiled and hugged Mom back. "I love you, too."

Chapter 10

Chicken Pox and Chicken Soup

One morning in early February, Rachel came down to breakfast scratching her arms. "I think there might be bugs in my bed," she complained.

Mom placed a kettle of water on the back of the stove and turned to face Rachel. "What makes you think that?"

Rachel pulled the sleeve of her nightgown up and held out her arm. "I have little bumps all over my arms, and they itch something awful!"

"Ach, my!" Mom exclaimed. "Those bumps aren't from any bugs, Rachel. I'm afraid you've got *wasserpareble* [chicken pox]."

"Wasserpareble?" Rachel repeated.

Mom nodded. "That's what it looks like."

"If you've got chicken pox, you'd better stay away from me," Jacob said as he entered the room. "I sure don't want them."

"I'll hold my breath so I won't blow any germs on you," Rachel said.

Mom patted Rachel's shoulder. "It's okay. Jacob had the chicken pox before you were born."

Jacob's eyebrows lifted. "I did?"

Mom nodded. "You, Henry, and Esther had them at the same time."

"Why didn't I get them?" Rachel wanted to know.

"You weren't born yet," Mom replied. "In fact, Jacob was just a boppli when they all came down with the chicken pox."

"What about you and Pap?" Rachel asked. "Have you had the chicken pox?"

Mom nodded. "Your daed and I had them when we were *kinner* [children]."

"What about Grandpa? I wouldn't want him to get sick because of me," Rachel said, shaking her head.

"Why would I get sick?" Grandpa asked as he entered the kitchen.

Rachel moved to the other side of the room. "I've got the wasserpareble, Grandpa. So if you haven't had them, don't get close to me."

Grandpa chuckled. "No worries, Rachel. I had chicken pox when I was a boy."

Rachel breathed a sigh of relief. At least she didn't have to worry about spreading any chicken pox germs on her family.

Mom looked at Jacob, and then at Rachel. "Has anyone at school had the chicken pox lately?"

Jacob shrugged. "Not that I know of."

"No one in class has been sick for several weeks," Rachel put in.

Mom peered at Rachel over the top of her glasses. "How do you feel? Does your throat hurt? Do you ache anywhere?"

"No, but I feel warm—and very itchy," Rachel said.

Mom touched Rachel's forehead. "I think you're running a fever." She turned back to the stove. "I'll fix some tea and toast and bring it to your room on a tray."

"Why can't I eat breakfast down here?"

"Because you're sick and need to be in bed where you can rest." Mom shook her head. "No school for you today, Rachel. Not until you're completely well."

"I don't want to miss school," Rachel wailed. "We're supposed to work on our valentines today. The school party is next week, you know."

"I'm afraid you'll have to work on yours at home," Mom said. "Now, scoot upstairs and get into bed. I'll bring your breakfast tray up soon."

Rachel swallowed around the lump in her throat and shuffled out of the kitchen. She didn't want to be sick. She wanted to go to school.

Fighting tears of frustration, Rachel climbed the stairs to her room and crawled into bed. She lay there, staring at the ceiling and wishing she could bring Cuddles into her room to comfort her.

"How do you feel, Rachel?" Mom asked when she entered Rachel's bedroom.

"I feel awful." Rachel tried to sit up, but her head started to pound. She sank back into the pillow with a moan. "Now I've got a *koppweh* [headache], and my arms itch terribly."

"Try not to scratch. That will leave scars." Mom set the tray she carried on the small table beside Rachel's bed and moved to Rachel's dresser. "These should help," she said as she removed a pair of dark stockings.

"What are those for?" Rachel asked. "If I can't go to school and have to stay in bed, why do I need to wear stockings?"

"They're not for your feet. They're to put over your hands so you won't scratch the pox marks." Mom slipped one stocking over Rachel's right hand and one over her left hand. "That should help. Now I'm going back downstairs to make some comfrey tea to put on your pox."

Rachel squinted. "Why would you put tea on my pox?"

"The tea is supposed to help them not itch so much." Mom patted Rachel's hand. "As soon as the tea is cool, I'll be back."

When Mom left the room, Rachel rolled onto her side. Tears trickled down her cheeks. *Why do I always have so much trouble?*

Rachel spent the next several days in bed, trying not to scratch, and feeling sorry for herself. Besides the fact that she would miss the valentine party at school on Friday, she would also miss the spelling bee. Since spelling was Rachel's favorite subject, she felt grouchy about having to stay home from school. Mom had reminded Rachel several times that she needed to learn more patience and that some things weren't in her control. However, Rachel was determined to get out of bed and prove she was doing better.

Screetch. . .screetch. A scratching sound at the window drew Rachel's attention. It had to be Cuddles, begging to get in.

Rachel pushed her covers aside and crawled out of bed. Her body ached, and her muscles felt like limp, wet noodles. With a shaky hand she lifted the window shade. Sure enough, Cuddles was perched on a tree branch outside Rachel's window.

As soon as Rachel opened the window, Cuddles leaped into her arms.

Rachel smiled. It was comforting to hold Cuddles and listen to her purr. Rachel knew Mom didn't like the cat on her bed, but she couldn't resist lying down with Cuddles in her arms. After a while, the cat crawled to the bottom of the bed and fell asleep.

Maybe if I go downstairs and find something to do, I'll feel better, Rachel thought. She slipped into her robe and slippers then tiptoed out of the room, so she wouldn't disturb Cuddles.

When Rachel entered the kitchen, the delicious aroma of chicken soup tickled her nose, and made her stomach rumble.

"Rachel, what are you doing out of bed?" Mom asked.

"I thought I should make some valentine hearts—in case I'm well enough to go to school on Friday."

Mom shook her head. "You won't be well enough. You should be back in bed."

"Oh, please, Mom. I promise I'll sit quietly at the table and work on my valentines. If I get tired, I'll go straight back to bed."

"Oh, all right," Mom finally agreed. "But you won't be up to going back to school on Friday. Jacob can take the valentines you make for the scholars, and then bring the ones home that they've made for you."

Rachel found some red and white paper, scissors, glue, and a black marking pen in Mom's craft drawer. She carried them to the table and sat down. She wouldn't admit it to Mom, but she was already tired.

She sat there several minutes, breathing slowly and rubbing her forehead.

"Does your head hurt?" Mom asked.

"Just a bit."

"Maybe you should go back up to bed and forget the valentines for now."

"I'll be all right." Rachel picked up the scissors and a piece of red paper; then she cut out a heart.

Mom went back to stirring the pot of soup. "I think this is done. Would you like a bowl of chicken soup, Rachel?"

"Jah, I would," Rachel replied.

Mom ladled some soup into a bowl and set it on the table. "Be careful not to spill soup on your valentines," she said.

"Aren't you going to have some?" Rachel asked.

"I was planning to eat lunch after your daed and grandpa get back from town, but the soup smells so good, I think I'll join you." Mom ladled some soup into another bowl and started across the room. She was almost to the table when Cuddles streaked into the kitchen and zipped over Mom's foot. Mom stumbled, bumped into a chair, and—*splat!*—her bowl of soup splattered all over the table!

Rachel jumped up. "My valentines—they're ruined!"

Mom pointed to Cuddles, who sat on the floor licking some of the spilled soup. "I didn't let the cat in the house. How do you suppose she got in?"

"I—I brought her inside," Rachel admitted. "She was in the tree outside my window, scratching to get in."

"Please don't tell me she was on your bed again."

Rachel nodded slowly as her head began to pound, and the room started to spin.

"Rachel, how many times have I told you—"

"I—I feel so dizzy." Rachel reached for the back of the chair, and Mom grabbed her arm.

"I knew you shouldn't have gotten up so soon." Mom guided Rachel toward the steps. "Back to bed with you now."

"What about my soggy valentine hearts?"

"I'll clean up the mess after I tuck you into bed."

Rachel spent the rest of the afternoon feeling sorry for herself. Not only had she disobeyed Mom and let Cuddles sleep on her bed, but now all her valentines were ruined. She wouldn't have any to send to school with Jacob.

Tap-tap-tap. Someone knocked on Rachel's bedroom door.

"Come in," she said with a sigh.

Esther poked her head inside the door. "Would you like some company?"

Rachel shrugged. "I suppose."

Esther sat in the chair by Rachel's bed. "I went to town this morning and decided to drop by on my way home to see how you feel."

Rachel scrunched up her nose. "I feel baremlich."

"That's understandable," Esther said with a nod. "Everyone feels terrible when they're grank."

"I'm not feeling terrible because I'm sick." Rachel pushed herself to a sitting position and leaned against the pillows. "I feel terrible because Mom spilled soup on my valentine hearts, and now they're ruined." She sniffed. "And I feel terrible because I can't go to school on Friday."

"If you went to school you might expose everyone to

the chicken pox," Esther said.

"I know, but if I stay home I'll miss the spelling bee and the Valentine's Day party." Tears welled in Rachel's eyes, and she blinked to keep them from spilling over.

Esther patted Rachel's hand. "You'll have other spelling bees, and I'm sure Jacob will bring your valentines home."

Rachel's chin quivered. "I wish I could do something to get well quicker."

"Just rest in bed, and do everything Mom says. Be patient and you'll be well before you know it."

"But not before Friday." Rachel nearly choked on the words.

"You need to relax and put your hope in the Lord, like the Bible says we should do," Esther said.

"Where does it say that?"

"In Isaiah 40:31, it says: 'But those who hope in the Lord will renew their strength. They will soar on wings like eagles; they will run and not grow weary, they will walk and not be faint.'"

"I almost fainted when I was in the kitchen," Rachel said.

"That's because you should have been in bed resting. You're not ready to be up for a long time yet." Esther gently squeezed Rachel's arm. "I'm going downstairs to help Mom make some pretty valentine hearts so Jacob can take them to school for you on Friday."

Rachel smiled. "Danki, Esther."

"Gern gschehne," Esther replied before she slipped out the door.

Rachel pulled the covers under her chin. It was nice to have a kind, helpful sister.

Chapter 11

Worst Day Ever

Slow down, Rachel. If you're not careful, you'll slip and fall," Jacob called as Rachel hurried on the snowy path leading to the schoolhouse. "What's the rush?"

"I'm anxious to get to school so I can get my valentines." Rachel turned to face Jacob. "The ones *you* forgot to bring home for me."

Jacob scrunched up his nose. "You should be glad I remembered to take the valentines to school that Mom and Esther made for you to give the others."

"Well," Rachel said, lifting her chin, "that was only because on the day of the party, Mom put them in a plastic bag and handed them to you on your way out the door."

Jacob shrugged. "At least they got there."

"But I still don't have *my* valentines."

"You'll get them when you get to school!" Jacob tromped past Rachel, kicking powdery snow all over her dress. "Hurry up, slowpoke. You'll make me late."

Rachel gritted her teeth. She wondered if Jacob would ever stop making fun of her. When they were both old and gray, would he still tease and call her names?

"Have you had any luck training Buddy?" Rachel asked, deciding they needed to change the subject.

Jacob shook his head. "Not yet. I think I may give up on the whistle and try to train Buddy on my own."

"I don't care how you train him, but you'd better think of something before my cat gets hurt."

"Buddy hasn't hurt Cuddles yet, Rachel. I've told you before, Buddy just wants to play."

"Even if that's true, I don't like it when he chases Cuddles, and neither does she!"

Jacob nudged Rachel's arm. "You worry too much, little bensel."

Ignoring Jacob's teasing, Rachel trudged on. When she entered the schoolhouse, she was surprised to see that no valentines were inside her desk.

She glanced around the room. Maybe Orlie or one of the other boys had hidden her valentines. If she'd had time, she would have asked some of the scholars if they knew anything about the valentines. But Elizabeth had already opened her Bible to read the morning scripture.

When the Bible reading was over, the children stood and repeated the Lord's Prayer and then sang. As soon as they returned to their seats, Rachel raised her hand. Elizabeth and her helper didn't seem to notice; they were busy handing out everyone's arithmetic papers.

Rachel hoped she could ask about the valentines when Sharon came by her desk, but when Sharon handed Rachel her arithmetic lesson, she hurried up the aisle before Rachel could speak.

Tap-tap-tap. Rachel tapped her pencil on the edge of her desk and stared at the arithmetic problems. Thanks to the itchy chicken pox, she'd been out of school almost two weeks. Even though she'd done some schoolwork at home, she hadn't spent much time on arithmetic. She hoped she could do all the problems.

"*Psst. . .*"

Rachel glanced across the aisle at her cousin Mary.

"You'd better get your lesson done," Mary whispered. "If you don't, you won't get to go outside for morning recess."

Rachel nodded. Mary was right. If she didn't finish her assignment before ten o'clock, she would probably have to skip recess in order to finish it.

Rachel picked up her pencil again. Between every problem she glanced at the clock on the wall. It was hard to be patient when she wanted to see her valentines.

Rachel finished the last problem just as Elizabeth announced that it was time to turn in their papers. Rachel handed her arithmetic paper to Sharon. She was getting ready to ask about her valentines when Sharon hurried off.

Maybe I won't go outside for recess, Rachel decided.

While others are playing in the snow, I'll look through everyone's desk for my valentines.

After the children's papers were collected, Elizabeth said it was time for recess.

Everyone scurried to the back of the room to get their coats, gloves, and hats, but Rachel stayed at her desk.

"Aren't you going outside?" Mary asked, coming to stand beside Rachel.

Rachel shook her head. "I'd rather stay in here, where it's warm."

"Are you feeling all right? You're not still feeling grank, are you?"

"I'm not sick. I just want to stay inside."

Mary shrugged and rushed out the door.

Rachel waited until Elizabeth and Sharon went outside; then she hurried to the first desk on the right side of the room and lifted the lid. There were several books, a shriveled apple, and two pencils, but no sign of her valentine cards.

Rachel moved on. She found no valentines in the next desk, either. She went up the row, lifting lids and looking inside every desk. She was ready to move to the next row, when the door swung open.

"Rachel, what are you doing?"

Bam! Rachel slammed the lid on the desk and faced her teacher. "I—I was looking for my valentines."

"In someone else's desk?"

Rachel nodded. "When I didn't find the valentines in my desk, I thought maybe someone had taken the valentines and hidden them."

Elizabeth shook her head. "I put your valentines in my desk."

"That's good to hear," Rachel said with a smile. "Can I please have them?"

"Sorry, Rachel," Elizabeth said, "but I won't give them to you until school ends this afternoon."

Rachel's smile turned to a frown. "How come?"

"For one thing, there's some candy in your sack of cards. I don't want you to be tempted to eat any now and spoil your lunch."

Rachel smiled. She hadn't even realized she might get candy with her valentines. "I won't eat too many," she said.

Elizabeth shook her head. "You'll have to wait until after school."

Rachel knew better than to argue. She didn't want to stay after school or have to take another note home to Mom and Pap. "Guess I'll go outside and play," she said with a sigh.

Elizabeth pointed to the clock. "We only have a few minutes left of recess—not enough time for you to go outside." She started to walk away, but turned back around. "One more thing, Rachel. . .no more snooping in other people's desks."

"I won't, Teacher; I promise."

As Rachel and Jacob walked home from school, Rachel stopped every few feet, reached into her sack of valentines, and pulled out a piece of candy.

"You're gonna be too full for supper if you keep eating like that," Jacob said.

"No, I won't." Rachel popped a piece of taffy into her mouth. "Ouch! I bit my tongue!"

"That's what you get for trying to eat so much candy at once." Jacob shook his finger at her. "Why don't you slow down and quit being so ungeduldich?"

"I'm not impatient."

"Jah, you are."

Rachel decided not to argue. It was more fun to eat her candy.

By the time they reached home, most of Rachel's candy was gone. "I don't feel well," she complained as they stepped onto the porch.

"What's wrong?" Jacob asked.

She held her stomach and groaned. "I've got a *bauchweh* [stomachache]."

The skin around Jacob's blue eyes crinkled when he frowned at her. "After all that candy you ate, I'm not surprised that your stomach hurts."

"You don't have to be mean."

"I'm not. I'm just stating facts."

Rachel was getting ready to respond, when—*zip!*—her cat raced past. *Zip! Zip!* Jacob's dog was on the cat's tail.

"Buddy, stop!" Rachel shouted. "Leave my cat alone!"

Whoof! Buddy lunged for Cuddles. *Whish!*—Cuddles scurried up the nearest tree.

Buddy pawed at the trunk of the tree. *Woof! Woof!*

"Get your *dumm* [dumb] dog!" Rachel shouted. She'd forgotten all about her stomachache. Her only concern was for Cuddles.

"Buddy's not dumb. He's a very schmaert dog." Jacob reached into his jacket pocket and pulled out the whistle. "Maybe he'll respond this time." He blew on the whistle. "Come here, Buddy!"

Buddy tipped his head back and howled. *Aw-oo-oo!*

"Jah, Buddy's schmaert all right—schmaert and dumm at the same time. He's smart enough to chase my cat up a tree and too dumb to know what to do when you blow that whistle." Rachel frowned. "If Cuddles gets stuck up there, it'll be your fault, Jacob!"

"She's not going to get stuck."

"How do you know?"

"Because she's a cat, and cats climb trees."

"I don't see what that proves."

Jacob grunted. "If the cat went up the tree, she'll come back down."

Rachel looked up. Cuddles sat on one of the highest branches. The poor thing looked so pathetic.

Woof! Woof! Woof! Buddy continued to bark while he pawed at the tree.

"Get down, Buddy! Go away!" Rachel scolded.

"I'll take him to the barn," Jacob said. He grabbed

Buddy's collar and led him away.

"Here, Cuddles. Come, kitty, kitty," Rachel begged her frightened cat. "That mean old dog is gone now. It's safe for you to come down."

Meow! Cuddles trembled.

Rachel shivered. It was cold outside and she wanted to go into the house where it was toasty. She thought Cuddles needed to go inside, too. "Please, Cuddles, come to me."

Meow! Meow!

"I know what I'll do!" Rachel set her backpack and sack full of valentines on the porch. Then she hurried to the barn.

"Did your cat come out of the tree?" Jacob asked as he closed the door to the stall where he kept Buddy.

She shook her head. "Not yet. I came in here to get Cuddles's food dish."

"Why?"

"To coax her down."

Jacob frowned. "If you leave her alone, she'll come down on her own."

"What if she doesn't?"

"She will."

"But she may not, so I'm going to help her." Rachel picked up Cuddles's dish and started for the barn door.

"Why do you have to be so impatient?" Jacob called. "You can't control every situation, you know!"

Rachel ignored Jacob and kept walking. When she

came to the tree where Buddy had chased Cuddles, she looked up. The cat still sat there, looking more frightened than before.

"This is my worst day ever," Rachel mumbled.

"You say that every day," Jacob said, joining her in front of the tree.

"Do not."

"Do so."

Rachel didn't feel like arguing. She had more important things on her mind. "Maybe I should climb the tree and bring Cuddles down," she said.

Jacob shook his head. "Don't be silly. That tree is too high for you to climb, and it could be dangerous."

"I'm not afraid."

"You should be."

Mom came out of the house. "I thought I heard voices." She looked at Rachel. "What's going on?"

"Jacob's dog chased my cat up the tree." Rachel pointed upwards. "Now Cuddles can't get down."

"She *can* get down," Jacob said.

"No, she can't."

"Can, too."

"I'm sure Cuddles will come down when she's ready." Mom stepped off the porch and touched Rachel's shoulder. "Why don't you and Jacob come inside and have hot chocolate and cookies?"

"That sounds good," Jacob quickly replied.

"What about you, Rachel?" Mom asked. "Are you

hungry for peanut butter cookies?"

"Rachel's not hungry for anything," Jacob said. "She's got a bauchweh from eating too much candy."

Rachel squinted at Jacob. *"Blappermaul* [blabbermouth]."

"Where did you get candy, Rachel?" Mom questioned.

"From school. It was in the sack with my valentines Jacob kept forgetting to bring home."

"She got so impatient that she ate all the candy on the walk home," Jacob said.

"I didn't eat it all." Rachel pointed to the sack on the porch. "I still have a few pieces left."

Mom clucked her tongue. "You know better than to eat too much candy, Rachel."

"I tried not to, Mom, but it tasted so good."

"If you've got a bauchweh, then you don't need any cookies," Mom said. "But you should get inside out of this cold."

"I'll be there in a few minutes." Rachel lifted the bowl of cat food and pointed to the tree. "I'm hoping Cuddles will get hungry. I want to see if she'll come down when she sees this food."

Mom nodded. "All right, but don't stay out here too long."

Jacob nudged Rachel with his elbow. "Only a little bensel would stand out here in the cold, staring at a cat in a tree." He snickered and followed Mom into the house.

Rachel ground her teeth together. *A lot Jacob knows. He can't even train his dog. I'll show him I'm not a silly child!*

Rachel set the cat food on the ground and rushed back to the barn. From behind Buddy's stall she heard, *Arf! Arf!*

Rachel held her hands over her ears. "Be quiet, Buddy!" She was glad the door to the stall was closed. The last thing she needed was Buddy jumping on her.

Buddy kept barking and scratched the stall door.

"You're not coming out," Rachel shouted as she spotted the small stepladder.

With a joyous bark, Buddy leaped over the stall door and bounded up to Rachel. "Bad dog! I hope Pap builds a doghouse and pen for you soon." She grunted. "Better yet, I hope Jacob decides to find you another home!"

Buddy wriggled and wagged his tail. Apparently he didn't realize she was irritated with him.

Rachel grabbed Buddy's collar and led him back to the stall. "Stay in here!" She slammed the door. Then she left the barn, dragging the ladder behind her.

When Rachel reached the tree, she positioned the ladder below one of the branches and put her foot on the first rung. One. . .two. . .three steps. . .she began to climb the ladder. When she reached the top rung, she stepped onto the branch. "I'm coming, Cuddles!"

Chapter 12

Self-Control

The wind whistled through the tree as Rachel stepped from one branch to the other, until she was right under Cuddles. She reached out her hand. "Here, Cuddles. Come, kitty, kitty."

"Rachel Yoder, what do you think you're doing?"

Rachel jumped at the sound of Pap's deep voice.

Meow! Rachel's cat shrieked and leaped from the tree.

"Cuddles!" Quickly, Rachel started back down the tree. As she took her first step, her dress snagged on a branch. She reached down to pull it loose, but lost her footing.

Rachel wobbled back and forth and grabbed the branch overhead, her heart pounding so hard she could hear it roar in her ears. Her fingers were cold and stiff, and it was hard to hold the branch. Suddenly, her hand slipped and her knees buckled. "Heeelp!" Rachel tumbled toward the ground.

Oomph! Rachel's arm smacked into the wooden ladder. Her lungs felt like all the air had been squeezed out as she dropped into a mound of snow.

Pap rushed to Rachel's side and knelt beside her. "Rachel, are you hurt?"

When Rachel tried to stand a searing pain shot through her right arm. "My arm—it hurts so much!"

"Let's get inside where it's warm." Pap scooped Rachel into his arms and started up the porch steps.

"What about Cuddles?" Rachel's eyes had teared up so much she couldn't see a thing. "Is—is Cuddles hurt?"

"Your cat's fine," Pap said. "When she fell from the tree, she landed on her feet. Then she took off for the barn."

Mom greeted them at the door. "What happened to Rachel?"

"She fell from the maple tree. I think she may have broken her arm," Pap said as he placed Rachel on the living room sofa.

Mom gasped. "What were you doing in the tree, Rachel?"

"I—I was trying to get Cuddles, but then she jumped, and—" Rachel's voice broke on a sob.

When Pap examined Rachel's arm, she tried not to cry. It wasn't easy to be brave when she hurt so badly.

"It's starting to swell, and I'm pretty sure Rachel's arm is broken," Pap said, looking up at Mom. "We'll need to call one of our English neighbors for a ride to the hospital."

Mom nodded.

"I don't want to go to the hospital!" Rachel wailed. She didn't care about being brave anymore. She was worried about what they might do to her at the hospital.

Mom put her hand on Rachel's shoulder. "Calm down, daughter. If your arm is broken, you'll need to have it set and put in a cast."

Grandpa stepped into the room, followed by Jacob and Henry. They all crowded around the sofa and stared at Rachel.

"What happened?" Henry asked.

"She fell from the maple tree," Pap explained.

Jacob grunted. "I told you not to climb up there, Rachel."

Rachel cried harder. She felt bad enough; did Jacob have to make her feel worse?

"Henry, run to the Johnsons' and see if they can take us to the hospital," Pap said. "Rachel will need her arm X-rayed to see if it's broken."

"I—I don't want to go," Rachel cried.

"It'll be all right," Mom quietly said. "The doctors and nurses will take care of you. Everything will be just fine."

Later that day, Rachel and her parents returned from the hospital. Rachel wore a pink cast on her arm, and Mom and Pap wore relief on their faces.

"How'd things go at the hospital?" Jacob asked as he

sat on the sofa beside Rachel.

"Everything went fine, but I'll have to wear my cast for six whole weeks," she replied. "I also have to be careful not to get it wet."

Jacob patted Rachel's left arm. "Six weeks isn't so bad. The time will go quicker than you think."

"There are so many things I can't do with only one arm—especially since I'm right-handed." Rachel frowned. "If I had to break an arm, why couldn't it have been the left one?"

"There are still many things you can do." Mom handed Rachel a pain pill the doctor had given her. "The more you use your left hand, the better you'll get at it."

Rachel popped the pill in her mouth and gulped some water. Then she turned to Jacob and said, "If that *mupsich* [stupid] dog of yours hadn't chased my cat up the tree, I wouldn't have a broken arm."

Jacob grunted. "Buddy's not stupid, and if you hadn't climbed the tree, you wouldn't have fallen. And if you hadn't fallen, you wouldn't have—"

"Your brother's right, Rachel," Pap interrupted. "You should have waited for Cuddles to come down on her own."

Rachel sniffed. "I never seem to do anything right."

"That's not true, Rachel," Grandpa said as he sat in the rocking chair and propped his feet on a footstool near the fireplace. "You do lots of good things, but you need to learn to have more patience and self-control."

She nodded as tears filled her eyes.

Mom handed Rachel a tissue. "Now dry your eyes and get ready for a surprise."

"Surprise?" Rachel loved surprises. "What's the surprise, Mom?"

Mom smiled and motioned to Pap. "Your daed's decided to make homemade ice cream for dessert tonight."

Rachel's eyebrows shot up. "Homemade ice cream in the middle of winter?"

"Jah, sure," Pap said with a chuckle. "Cold, creamy, vanilla ice cream tastes wunderbaar any time of the year."

Rachel nodded. "I love homemade ice cream!"

"And eating ice cream is something you can do with one arm," Henry added as he entered the room from the kitchen.

"While you and your mamm were in seeing the doctor, I called Esther and Rudy and told them what happened," Pap said. "I also invited them to join us for ice cream tonight."

"I'm glad you did. It's always nice to see Esther and Rudy," Rachel said with a smile. "Will Grandma and Grandpa Yoder come over, too?"

Pap shook his head. "Grandma came down with a bad cold yesterday, so she doesn't feel like going anywhere."

"I'm sure they'll come visit you as soon as Grandma feels better." Mom motioned to the sofa. "Do you want to stretch out here and rest until supper? Or would you rather go to your room?"

"If I stay here, can I have Cuddles with me?"

Mom hesitated but nodded. "I'll have Jacob bring her in."

Jacob frowned. "Why do I have to do it?"

"Because Rachel's not going out to the barn to look for the cat," Pap said.

"She might slip and fall on the ice," Grandpa added. "You wouldn't want that to happen, would you, Jacob?"

"No, of course not." Jacob started for the door, but turned back around. "Can I bring Buddy in the house, too?"

"No!" everyone shouted.

"Just thought I'd ask." Jacob shrugged and hurried out the door.

"I think Henry and I had better head outside, too," Pap said. "We have some chores to do." He smiled at Mom. "We'll be back in plenty of time for supper."

Mom smiled. "Since we got home from the hospital so late, we'll just have soup and sandwiches for supper."

When Pap and Henry headed outside, Grandpa left his rocking chair and picked up a paper sack that had been lying on the table near the sofa. "After you left for the hospital, I found this on the porch." He placed the sack in Rachel's lap. "I believe your valentine cards from school are inside."

Rachel peered into the sack and nodded. She'd forgotten about her valentine cards. "Can I have a piece of candy?" she asked.

Mom shook her head. "I think you had enough

candy earlier, don't you?"

"I guess I did." Rachel thought about the stomachache she'd had after eating too much candy. As bad as her stomach had hurt, it didn't compare to the pain she'd felt when she'd hit the ladder and broken her arm. She wouldn't have had that stomachache if she hadn't eaten too much candy, and she wouldn't have broken her arm if she hadn't climbed the tree.

Mom kissed Rachel's forehead. "I'll let you look at your valentines while I go to the kitchen and heat some soup."

"Okay, Mom."

Grandpa sat at the end of the sofa. "Would you like me to rub your feet while you read your valentines, Rachel?"

"Jah, sure. That would feel good." Rachel nestled against the sofa cushions and took a drink of water. It was nice to be treated special. Maybe the next six weeks wouldn't be so bad after all.

That evening after supper, Rudy and Esther showed up.

"You're right on time," Pap said, winking at Rudy. "I was about to begin cranking the ice cream."

Rudy chuckled. "Then you'll need another pair of strong arms to help."

Pap nodded. "Usually Rachel gets the first chance to crank, but since she only has one good arm and needs to rest, we men will have to do the cranking ourselves." He smiled at Rachel, who sat on the sofa with Cuddles draped across her lap.

"How do you feel?" Esther asked. "Does your arm hurt much?"

"A little, but the medicine the doctor gave me for pain helps." Rachel yawned. "It also makes me sleepy."

"Don't fall asleep yet," Mom said. "The ice cream will be ready to eat soon." She motioned to the kitchen. "That is, if our men ever start cranking."

"I guess we've had our orders." Grandpa smiled at Pap. "If you don't mind, Levi, I'd like to be the first one to crank."

"Don't mind at all." Pap patted Rachel's knee. "Don't fall asleep now, you hear?"

She grinned. "I won't, Pap."

When the men left the room, Mom sat in the rocking chair, and Esther sat on the couch beside Rachel. She touched Rachel's cast. "Rudy and I were sorry to hear about your accident. It's a good thing this happened to you during the winter."

"Why's that?" Rachel asked.

"If it had happened during spring, summer, or autumn, you wouldn't have had the snow to break your fall." Esther's forehead wrinkled. "You could have been hurt worse."

"I guess that's true." Rachel glanced at her cast and sighed. "I wish I hadn't been foolish enough to climb that tree. I guess that's what I get for being so impatient."

"Sometimes we learn lessons the hard way," Mom said.

Rachel nodded. "Grandpa says I should practice *self-control* instead of trying to *be in control*."

"Grandpa's right," Mom agreed.

"Changing the subject," Esther said with a smile. "I have some good news for you, Rachel."

"What's that?" Rachel was always eager to hear good news.

"Rudy and I are going to have a boppli."

Rachel's mouth dropped open. "Really? When will the baby be born?"

"Early October."

"That's just a few months after Mom's supposed to have her boppli." Rachel looked at Mom. "Did you know Esther was expecting a baby?"

"Jah. Esther told me a few days ago, but she asked me not to say anything, because she wanted to tell you."

Esther smiled. "Are you happy about becoming an aunt, Rachel?"

"I'm happy if you are," Rachel replied.

"I truly am, and so is Rudy. He hopes it will be a buwe, but I'm hoping for a *maedel* [girl]." Esther continued to talk about how she couldn't wait to become a mother, and how much fun it would be when her baby and Mom's baby were old enough to play together.

Mom's voice blended with Esther's, and soon Rachel noisily yawned as her head lulled against the pillows. *In a few months, I'm going to be a big sister and an aunt.* Her eyes shut. *I wonder if the babies will be boys or girls.*

"Wake up, Rachel! The ice cream is ready!"

Rachel's eyes snapped open, and she sat up with a start. Jacob's face was a few inches from hers. "Don't scare me like that," she said.

"I wanted you to know the ice cream's ready."

"You didn't have to yell."

"How else could I wake you?"

Mom nodded toward the kitchen. "Jacob, why don't you help Pap dish up the ice cream? Then you can bring it in here for us."

"Jah, okay." Jacob scurried out of the room.

A few minutes later, he returned with two bowls of ice cream. He handed one to Rachel and gave one to Mom. Rudy came in next, with two bowls—one for him and one for Esther. Then Pap and Henry arrived, each carrying their bowls of ice cream. Finally, Grandpa showed up with two bowls. He gave one to Jacob and kept one for himself.

"This looks appeditlich," Rachel said, smacking her lips. She placed the bowl on her lap, and using her left arm, dipped the spoon into the creamy ice cream. "Yum. It *is* delicious!" She took another bite, and then another. The ice cream tasted so good, she couldn't eat it fast enough.

Zing! Rachel dropped the spoon into the bowl and gasped as she grabbed her forehead.

"What's wrong?" Mom rushed over to Rachel. "Does your arm hurt again?"

Rachel drew in a deep breath and shook her head. "It's not my arm. I—I had a brain freeze."

"That's because you were eating too fast," Henry said. "I always get that when I eat ice cream too quickly."

"I'll take smaller bites," Rachel said.

When Rachel finished her ice cream, she was going to ask for a second bowl, but changed her mind. She remembered how her stomach had hurt after she'd eaten too much candy, so she knew it would be better if she stopped eating before she made herself sick.

"This has been nice," Rudy said, "but it's getting late, and it's time for Esther and me to head home."

Esther nodded. "I'm sure Rachel is ready to go to bed."

Rachel yawned. She could barely keep her eyes open.

Rudy and Esther gathered their coats and said good-bye.

"Is it all right if I go to the barn and say goodnight to Buddy?" Jacob asked as Mom gathered everyone's empty bowls.

"You'll need to go to bed soon, but I guess you can go to the barn for a few minutes," Mom replied.

Jacob raced for the door, and just as his fingers touched the knob, Mom called, "Before you go to the barn, please go to the chicken coop and see if there are any eggs."

Jacob's forehead wrinkled. "How come?"

"Your daed used the last of our eggs to make the ice

cream," Mom said. "I'll need more for breakfast."

Rachel listened to see what Jacob would say. She knew he didn't like to collect eggs.

To Rachel's surprise, Jacob smiled and said, "Sure, Mom, I'll get those eggs right away." He rushed out the door.

Mom turned to Rachel and said, "It's been a long day, hasn't it?"

Rachel nodded and pointed to her cast. "A long and painful day."

"Things will get better as your arm begins to heal." Mom stroked Rachel's cheek. "And the medicine the doctor gave you will help with the pain."

Rachel stared at the fireplace across the room. Orange and red flames lapped at the logs as they crackled and popped. Her eyelids grew heavy again, and she started to doze.

"Let's go upstairs, and I'll help you get ready for bed," Mom said, tapping Rachel's shoulder.

Rachel nodded and stood. She and Mom were almost to the stairs when the back door opened, and Jacob burst into the hallway. His face was red as a cherry, and gooey, broken eggs shells covered his jacket.

Mom's mouth dropped open. "Ach, Jacob! What happened?"

"I was in such a hurry to gather the eggs so I could get to the barn to see Buddy that I forgot to carry an egg basket to the chicken coop." Jacob drew in a breath and blew it out quickly. "I tried to carry the eggs inside my coat, but then I slipped on a patch of ice and all the eggs broke."

"Are you hurt?" Mom asked with concern.

Jacob shook his head. "Just the eggs."

Rachel chuckled. "Guess I'm not the only one in the family who gets in a hurry to do things."

Jacob turned to Mom and said, "I'm sorry. Maybe I can find more eggs in the morning."

Mom nodded and pushed her glasses to the bridge of her nose. "This has been quite a day. I hope both of my kinner have learned a good lesson."

"I have," Rachel and Jacob said at the same time.

"Jacob, you'd better clean up, while I help Rachel get ready for bed," Mom said.

Jacob scurried to the bathroom as Rachel and Mom headed upstairs. A short time later, Rachel snuggled beneath the cozy quilt on her bed. She was almost asleep when the bedroom door opened and Grandpa poked his head into her room. "May I come in?"

"Of course," Rachel replied.

"I wanted to say goodnight." Grandpa stepped into the room, bent down, and kissed Rachel's forehead.

She smiled up at him. "I love you, Grandpa."

"I love you, too, Rachel." Grandpa moved to the window and lifted the shade. "It's snowing again. If we get another blizzard, you may not be able to go school tomorrow."

"That's okay." Rachel smiled. "I guess I can't do

anything about it. I think I'm learning my lesson Grandpa. When I try to be in control, I mess things up. The weather is out of my control. And so are many other things."

Rachel yawned and closed her eyes. "I'm thankful that God's in control of everything."

Recipe for Mrs. Yoder's Shoofly Pie

2 (8 inch) unbaked pie shells

Filling:
1 cup molasses
1 cup hot water
1 teaspoon baking soda
2 eggs, beaten
½ cup brown sugar

Crumb Mixture:
2 cups flour
¾ cup brown sugar
⅓ cup butter
½ teaspoon nutmeg
½ teaspoon cinnamon

Preheat oven to 400°. Combine molasses, hot water, and baking soda in a bowl. Add eggs and brown sugar. Divide half the mixture equally into the unbaked pie shells. Mix the ingredients for the crumb mixture in a separate bowl. Sprinkle half the crumb mixture over the filling in each of the pies. Add the second half of the filling to the pies, and sprinkle the last half of the crumb mixture over the top. Bake for 10 minutes at 400°; then reduce the heat to 350° for 50 minutes. Recipe makes two 8-inch pies.